Also by Alice Lichtenstein

The Genius of the World

LOST

A NOVEL

ALICE LICHTENSTEIN

SCRIBNER

New York   London   Toronto   Sydney

Scribner
A Division of Simon & Schuster, Inc.
1230 Avenue of the Americas
New York, NY 10020

First Scribner hardcover edition March 2010

SCRIBNER and design are registered trademarks of The Gale Group, Inc., used
under license by Simon & Schuster, Inc., the publisher of this work.

For information about special discounts for bulk purchases,
please contact Simon & Schuster Special Sales at
1-866-506-1949 or business@simonandschuster.com

The Simon & Schuster Speakers Bureau can bring authors to your live
event. For more information or to book an event, contact the
Simon & Schuster Speakers Bureau at 1-866-248-3049 or
visit our website at www.simonspeakers.com.

Designed by Carla Jayne Jones

Manufactured in the United States of America

3   5   7   9   10   8   6   4   2

Library of Congress Control Number: 2009037973

ISBN 978-1-4391-5982-8
ISBN 978-1-4391-7167-7 (ebook)

For my parents

"... One word frees us of all the weight and pain of life: that word is love."

—SOPHOCLES, *Oedipus at Colonus*

CONTENTS

Prologue

Corey

He should have been afraid, but he wasn't. He'd done the bad thing and the bad thing made nothing as bad ever since. Nothing really scared him all the way ever since the bad thing turned him inside out, inside out. Then that disappeared and this was left—the nothing, the nothing that wasn't so bad.

Still, touching the man's pocket made him hold his breath. Like he expected the man to jump. Like he expected a smell, which there was none, not much. Not like a farmer. Smell of cow flop like a man had messed his pants and didn't care. Farmers were like big shitty babies, spreading their smell around and not caring about anybody's business but their own.

His grandfather was a farmer and he smelled that way and didn't care.

The man just lay there, but still when he touched the coat he did it gingerly like the man might suddenly spring up, grab his arm. In the pocket he found nothing. Not a wallet. Or a match. Or a piece of change. Only a bit of grit, black grains which he wiped on his own pants.

The man was curled up, his coat open and what looked like a pajama shirt undone. But not quite like he was sleeping. More like he was running sideways across the hill and got pushed. The legs still running and the chin tucked, the shoulders twisted this-away.

The boy looked at the man's feet: sneakers cut low and ridiculous in the snow. Blue lightning bolts at the ankle; white cotton socks. Black treads packed with ice and stone. The boy told himself he wasn't afraid. He knew what happened to people when they died. People were just like animals, just like the doe he found in a winter field, jacked by some coward in a car and never picked up. And the porcupine by the side of the road. And the possum and the skunk. Their bellies got big and their tongues, too. Everything got big before it got small. And sometimes after a long time and sometimes in no time, the thing was eaten.

Last night he dreamt of his brother running toward him looking like a marshmallow burned black. When he tried to hold him, Lance crumpled to ash. The nightmare had sent him into the woods. He'd had the dream in the night, but all through the morning he saw his brother's black face; he heard his shriek.

After lunch, he ran into the woods, straight to the place he liked to go. A place the deer liked, too. Once he'd gotten up so early, he surprised them still sleeping in the long grass that poked through the snow. Up they sprang, leaving their pushed-down beds, their egg-shaped nests that cupped their bodies, held in their warmth. When he lay down in the shape, he imagined himself a fawn.

Now with the noon sun rising, the old man lay there. Corey felt his heart digging sharply beneath his ribs. Staring down at the man, running, sleeping, in the snow, he wished he could drop that way. Quick; no pain.

He glanced at the sky. Such a quiet, heavenly blue, but he had to get back. Start chores. Grandfather's nap would be over; he'd want him to clean something, fix something. He'd have to run all the way back to be on time. But something caught at him. He couldn't leave the old man like this. The man was a man, not a thing. He didn't like to think of him being eaten.

Beneath his fingertips, the man's cheek felt smooth and cold like harness leather; he wanted to cover him with something, something soft, a flannel blanket, a piece of cloth. He looked around. Bare sticks; thorn branches. Blown pinecones, bound tight as turds. There was only one thing he could think of. Here and there, scattered on the snow, were whisks of evergreen needles, drooping gracefully as a fox's tail. He picked up one and then another, another, and another. He laid the needled fans on the man's body. It wasn't much, but it was something.

PART I
FRIDAY

ONE

SHE WAKES TO HER OWN SHOUT. RIGHT THERE OUT IN THE open like a character in a book. "Christopher?"

His side of the bed is empty, the covers pushed back in a tangled wave, and suddenly Susan is aware of the sounds coming from the closet, thuds of shoes being kicked, jangling of empty hangers, muffled agony.

In an instant she has pushed aside her own covers, touched her bare feet to the soft carpet. The closet is a small room of its own with a door that folds back on itself like a fan.

"Christopher! Hold on. I'm here," she says as she fumbles with the tiny knobs, the flimsy panels. The closet light comes on as the doors open and there is her husband, hunkered in a nest of shirts, pants, ties.

He looks up at her with the wary, watchful eyes of a nocturnal animal coaxed into light. "Where thing loud you sit?" he asks.

"The toilet. You want the toilet."

Christopher nods, and she grabs his hand, pulling him gently to his feet. She is younger than he, and taller. And for a moment she has the sensation that she is pulling a child from a sandbox, a reluctant, drooping child. Peter, their son, who used to play for hours and hours on the monkey bars until she dragged him home.

The bathroom is small and narrow. The toilet sits at the far end, the vanity and sink beside it, the tub along one wall. Susan enters first, reaching for a hand towel above the sink, which she drapes over the medicine cabinet mirror, something she remembers the rabbi doing when he came to sit shiva for her mother. In this case it is so that Christopher will be not be startled by his image.

In the middle of the bathroom, Christopher halts, turns, backs himself to the edge of the receptacle like a man parking a semi. He reaches behind, feeling for the lid, the rim.

"You're there," she says as she turns on the sink faucet, a tip she'd read somewhere, to use the streaming faucet as a cue.

Christopher nods. With a faint grunt, he hooks his thumbs in the elastic waistband of his pajama pants, shoves them down.

In the old days, this is when she might venture downstairs alone to start their breakfast, while Christopher dabbed lotion on his face, shaved himself with a plastic razor. No more.

"That's great," she says, watching him slowly straighten to pull up his pants. His movements have become old even though he is not old, not really, barely seventy. She reaches behind him to flush the toilet, something he never remembers to do. Never *did* remember to do, she reminds herself. "Now wash hands."

He turns to her, surrendering his hands to hers. He has small, wiry hands, the hands of the builder he was before he became an architect.

"Soap, first." She slips the soap in and out of his cradled palms. "Rinse, next." He is not always this docile. Sometimes he calls her "the enemy," sometimes "the bitch." Sometimes when she takes his hands in hers, he pulls away as though her palms are on fire.

This morning he looks curious, a little afraid.

"Water," she says. "You used to love water. Swimming in water. This water is nice and warm." She squeezes his hands lightly, submerging them in the basin of warm water, then lets them go.

"Soft," Christopher says. "Clouds."

The water swirls with tiny air bubbles, a milky trail where he has waved his soapy hands to make what looks to Susan like a galaxy. "Beautiful."

He nods, though he looks confused, and Susan presses on the drain, hoping he won't startle at the croak and whirl of the water disappearing.

In the kitchen, Susan places a tablet of glyburide and a glass of water in front of Christopher at the table. "Here, while I make you an egg." Sometimes it is easy like this, Christopher swallowing his medicine without hesitation, an automatic response.

"Egg's good."

She watches him as he sets the glass down, then slides his clean hands into the box of buttons she keeps on the table to keep him occupied, something she read in a book. He scoops them up, lets them dribble through his fingers, then dives his fingertips in again. To her relief, he is smiling, absorbed. Content for the moment.

What is it her grandmother used to say? Buttons for memory. Why? Why buttons? Because they're so easy to lose?

She turns away humming a little tune. *Oh when the saints . . .* Perhaps it's not going to be such a bad day. The refrigerator door opens with a mild wheeze. The seal is weak, the plastic encrusted with some sort of dark scum she hasn't had time to clean off. When she bought the house, she bought the appliances, too. The old electric stove, which she loathes; this decrepit refrigerator; a dishwasher that can't be fixed. It was the easiest way; the fastest way. One of her mistakes. One of the many.

Peering into the refrigerator, she pushes aside a container of yogurt, a quart of milk, a brick of cheese, a half-eaten jar of rasp-berry fruit spread. No eggs. "Damn it." She shuts the refrigerator door.

Christopher looks up from his buttons.

"Nothing. Forgot to buy eggs. Cereal instead. Buttered toast. Or we can have some yogurt."

"Eggs stole? Stole? Who?"

Too many choices. Too many words. Christ. Once they were all about words. His province was the daily crossword puzzles; hers, the Sunday *Times*. Occasionally, she copied the daily puzzle at work and they lay in bed, shoulder to shoulder, racing. To her amazement, he often won. But more often they complemented each other: she knew all the Roman and Greek gods and god-desses; Christopher knew the songs.

"Not stolen. I forgot. I—forgot—to buy—eggs." Slow it down. Keep it simple.

"I want eggs. Christmas eggs."

That means he wants them wet, scrambled, running with cheese the way his mother used to make them. "Listen, we don't *have* eggs. I'll make oatmeal today; eggs, tomorrow."

"Christmas eggs."

Susan sighs, squeezing her temples between her thumb and forefinger. What now? Run for eggs? Drive to the café? An image comes to mind of a photograph she once saw of a man in the Dolomites, roping from the pinnacle of one rock spire to another, a man who looked as though he were swinging on a pulley along a high wire, and the caption read, "Timing is critical in this maneu-ver; one mistake means instant death." Christopher's medicine needs to be taken with food otherwise his blood sugar will start to lower. He needs to eat now.

Susan breathes deeply. "Here, a yogurt. To get started. Then we'll go get some eggs."

The second she puts the yogurt down, he sweeps it off the table with the back of his hand.

"Shit," she says, kneeling to retrieve the plastic cylinder whose lid she was smart enough to leave on. "Behave."

Christopher's mouth turns down, his chin drops. "Egg."

"All right, egg. We'll get in the car. We'll go to the café. Or the diner. Only we've got to be dressed. We're still not dressed." She looks down at her satin pajamas, a pale blue that makes her think of ice. Christopher looks almost boyish in his red plaid pajamas, his stocking feet. "Want to get dressed?"

Christopher nods, but as they cross the living room, he stops in front of the Christmas tree, planting his feet in a way she's seen before, as though gravity has increased tenfold.

"Come on. Going upstairs. Going to get dressed. Then we'll go out for breakfast. *Christmas breakfast.*" Though Christmas and New Year's passed over a week ago.

The tree is a blue spruce with shadowed needles and a pungent, woodsy smell that makes her yearn for a brisk walk in the outdoors. She put it up herself, acting on sheer willpower. Not that she cares much about Christmas trees: she comes from a family of socialists; she is Jewish. Christopher loves Christmas, though, has delighted in it since he was a child. Every Christmas Eve of their married life until Christopher got sick, they held a trimming party, a crackling fire in the granite hearth, trays of smoked salmon on squares of stiff Norwegian bread, and of course, Christopher the beaming host, mixing his famous Manhattans.

"Okay. Here." She twists an ornament from the tree. "Remember this one? Your mother gave it to you." A gnome on a cardboard square; pipe-cleaner legs, acorn body. How could it have lasted so long?

Christopher shakes his head as he reaches for a red metallic ball dangling chest high from a spiny twig. With both hands, he rubs the ball on his chest, polishing it like an apple.

"Take it easy," Susan warns, but even as she does, he is raising the shiny red ball toward his open mouth.

Susan leaps forward, batting the ornament away, her fingertips brushing the side of his mouth in a light slap. Christopher steps back. Both of them can hear the light metallic crunch of the ornament under his socked heel. A second later, he begins to howl.

"Oh God," Susan says. "I'm sorry." She would like to take a look at his foot, but as she reaches for him, he pushes her arm away.

Kneeling, she picks up the shards, iridescent as beetle shells. Behind her, Christopher curls up in his special chair, a light blue La-Z-Boy. She is fifty-seven, twelve years younger than Christopher. She was twenty-six when they married. Then his seniority seemed so comfortable, she tucked herself into it, a perfect fit. Her knees ache as she gets to her feet. Christopher is still in his chair, his howling reduced to quiet sobs. She dumps the handful of glass in the wastebasket, blowing gently across her palm to make sure the fine splinters are off. Then she goes over to Christopher.

"C'mon, lighten up." She slides her fingers down the back of his collar, pressing the bony lumps at the top of his spine, kneading the flanges of muscle on the sides of his neck. "Relax, now. It's okay. You're going to be okay." But even as she works to keep her voice even, under control, she can hear a raging voice in her head that could possess her at any moment. *Why can't this ever let up?* She gives Christopher's shoulders another rub, pats the top of his spine. Still he won't uncurl. "If you're going to be like that, I'm going to need to breathe."

She reaches into the cabinet beneath the television for her blue mat, which she unfurls with a great flap before settling it like a beach towel in the wind. She wasn't always this flexible of mind, one minute, getting dressed; the next minute, doing yoga. The disease has taught her this—seize the moment, the day, the hour.

As she lowers herself onto the mat, she catches a glimpse of Christopher getting up and heading for the stairs. *Follow him,* says the voice in her head. Her spine stiffens. In a minute. Then she'll zip into her clothes, get Christopher to the diner for eggs.

She slides the video into its slot, and the television screen blooms into peacock blue, a chorus of angels humming *Om.* Susan breathes deeply and sweeps her arms overhead, interlacing her fingers and stretching her inverted palms. She can feel the tug of her diaphragm lifting, separating her torso from the weight of her bottom and thighs. Ecstasy. In such a small movement. She can't fathom why. Her friend Molly Tyne chose this video for her. "The only one you'll find bearable," she said. "Minimal reverence required."

Aside from the mild affront that Molly thinks she *needs* something, Susan is grateful. It is true that in the mornings, her body is stiff as a board; her limbs crucified to their sockets. She should schedule a massage, find someone to realign her. But it's far too complicated with Christopher. He can't be parked like a car in a garage, or an infant at the nursery. Susan rolls her neck to one side, letting the weight of her skull stretch her neck muscles. "Breathe," says the yoga instructor, and Susan tries, though this is the hardest part for her, letting her abdomen balloon after years of being trained to "suck it in." "Let the breath fill up the lungs from the bottom, let the breath expand the torso."

Susan frowns, straightening her neck, squeezing the pouch of flesh over her abdomen as she begins to twist, lightly, keeping her back straight, lifting, gently twisting, until she can look back at the living room wall, a wan bone color, bare of photographs, of art of any kind. Keep things simple, the books say. Keep things uncluttered. A Zen monastery would be the perfect place to live with this disease. A Zen priest, the perfect caretaker.

On the video, the instructor is down on all fours, calling for "downward-facing dog," her rump sticking up in the air. Susan follows, letting her spine sag, tilting her sacrum skyward until she experiences a moment of abandon, of release. Her liberated buttocks expand, spread open, spread wide.

Without warning Christopher is against her, his bare calves, his stocking feet, his penis. "Hey—" she begins. She assumes playfulness on his part, though the Christopher she knew was never playful quite like this. "Cut it—"

He yanks down her pajama pants, her underwear. And she can tell from the tickle of his hairiness against her bottom that he is naked from the waist down. In one motion, she flips neatly on her back, shoves up at his chest to free herself, but she can't get up, her ankles are bound by her pants like a Chinese jump rope.

Christopher lowers himself on top of her, nudging her legs open.

What should she do? Knee him? Let him have his way? It happens sometimes that Christopher's lust thrusts itself out of nowhere, sparked by nothing, it seems, but testosterone releasing in his brain.

Christopher's hands press onto her shoulders, flattening them, as he lifts his chest, seeks her opening, like a soft blind animal that can't find its way. The air has suddenly become clotted with the smell of his sweat and hers. A drop of something, a tear, a splatter of drool, lands on her cheek and she would like to wipe it away, but can't. She can't see his face, only the skin of his neck, the pepper-and-white stubble, stretched taut over the knot of his throat. She reaches down, grasps his penis, guides it.

When he plunges into her, his moan is like a wolf's howl, all rage and release. And it strikes Susan that the pain between her legs is like the pain of giving birth and, perhaps, of dying, that lying here on her back, she has fulfilled Christopher's deepest wish—that no being has ever wanted anything more.

Two

Stepping out of the shower, Susan towels herself quickly, slips on clean underwear, a pair of slacks, and a turtleneck. She left the door open in case Christopher called out for her, but when she left him, he was sound asleep on the blue mat, his upper lip twitching as though he were dreaming a conversation he wished he could join.

Stealthy as a cat, she creeps down the carpeted stairs, hoping not to wake him. He still needs breakfast. He still needs his other meds. But she cannot jeopardize this chance to recover herself.

Beside him on the floor, she lays out a pair of tan pants, a pair of boxers, thinking it will be easier to dress him right there when he wakes up rather than have to bother with stairs again.

At the kitchen door, she reaches for her down coat, shoves her feet into her felt-lined boots. She'll just go down to the mailbox, she thinks. Fresh air will do her some good.

Outside, the sky is a hard, shimmering blue. The air is sharp. A new snow fell last night without her having been aware. Inhaling deeply, she wants to weep with gratitude for the natural world.

At the end of the driveway, black-capped chickadees dart in and out of the holly bush's glossy leaves. She and Christopher used to stand in their winter yard in Princeton for hours, waiting for the chickadees to trust their stillness and peck sunflower seeds from their mittened palms.

The mailbox is empty, she knew it would be, but something makes her feel as though she needs to mime opening and closing it. *You see, Judge, I was just getting the mail.* She looks up and down the empty road. The house is not far from town, but still remote. A forest of evergreens stretches along one side; meadows along the other.

She checks her watch. Two minutes. Surely she can take a little more time. She turns right at the end of the driveway. She'll walk up to the neighbor's box and around. A quarter of a mile; a half mile both ways. She needs the exercise.

She remembers the time she left Peter, their son, in the electric swing, purring and steady, sound asleep, thinking, He'll never know. She remembers walking backward at first, backward toward the front door as though she were unraveling something, as though she held a ball of string in her hand, unraveling as she went. An invisible tether.

A sense of mischief, of daring came over her. How bad could it be if the child woke up? He was buckled; he was safe (enough), though he might scream. Faster and faster the ball unraveled. She was tethered at the waist like a moon walker to the mother ship, but she was walking forward now, not backward, walking quickly around the block. She felt like tying surveyor's ribbons at every corner, to prove she'd been there.

When she got back, Peter was still asleep, his chin bent deeply toward his chest, a thread of drool spinning from lip to tiny knuckle.

She turned off the swing, sank to the sofa opposite, and wept noiseless tears of repentance and thanks.

She sighs. A half mile out, and back. She's got to walk. She just has to.

THREE

SHOULD HE TELL? THE WORDS BEAT IN COREY'S EARS AS HE ran back through the woods, pushing away branches that tried to snag him in their grasp for further questioning. He didn't want to tell anyone what he saw. If he told, they might blame him. They might say it was his fault, like when the fire started and the house burned down. The man might be dead, and they might blame him. Death followed him everywhere, he thought, so he wouldn't be surprised.

That's why he lived with his grandparents, because no one else in the family could stand the sight of him. He was the scar that reminded them of pain. Best for all of them that he should go away for a while, the judge said. His mother, his brother who remained, his aunt and his uncle, his teacher, and all the kids in his class agreed. Best to make him disappear like it had all disappeared.

Riding in the back of his grandparents' car, he'd seen the burned lot where his aunt and uncle's house had stood. Gone now. No house. No big tree in front with the swing hanging from it, no toys in the yard. The fence that he'd liked was gone. *Picket, picket, picket. Picket your nose and picket your butt. He and Lance picking and poking and rolling on the grass until tears had come.*

His aunt and uncle's house burned down. Right down to the ground. Their first and only house.

Now where it stood was a square of yellow grass on a dead-end street, across from the funeral home and up from the park, right beside the overpass. When he had slept overnight at his aunt and uncle's house, he liked to feel the rumble of the trucks in his bones, and to guess their size and weight and what they were carrying from where to where. His grandfather, driving slowly past, slowed further, but did not stop. "No one's gonna buy it," he said. And his grandmother echoed, "No one's gonna build on that lot."

His aunt was his mother's sister, who didn't have kids, and her husband was Bill, and he was okay because he worked at the hardware store and didn't drink. His uncle smoked, but so what. *If that's his worst habit,* his aunt used to say, shrugging. Uncle Bill was always losing his lighters and he and Lance were always finding them, but they didn't let on. They had an arsenal of lighters they kept in a shoe box. See-through tubes of blue, pink, purple, yellow, filled with clear fluid that sloshed back and forth, making tiny rolling seas.

His aunt and uncle had them over on nights when his mom worked, which was a lot. He and Lance had their own room in their house. A small one with cracks running everywhere and a dark yellow spot that spread on the ceiling when it rained. Still, a room in a real house, and what he liked about the house was it was wide and didn't make you sweat.

In his bunk at home in the trailer, he had dreams of being on a train, rattling down tracks and going he didn't know where. But in his aunt and uncle's house, he dreamt solid. Sometimes no dreams at all. Just folding into a blackness more delicious than cream.

It was Lance who started the game at their aunt and uncle's house. *Flicka the Bic,* his older brother said and snapped the lighter and flicked his wrist. *Flicka the Bic,* they challenged each other and their flames flew on, so soft and beautiful, like pussy willow buds. Only the blue was hot. He liked to stare at it. But Lance called him weird. *Flick the thing, boy. On guard.* So they'd duel, dancing forward and back, whirling their arms, whirling the flame.

The bad thing was he hadn't died. If he'd died like Lance had, it would have been a good thing. Everyone hated him now and loved his brother. When his uncle said *it was my fault,* his mother shut him up. *Nonsense. He knowed better.* His mother knew it was *his* fault. He believed her. But it wasn't on purpose, he might have said. The fire was so beautiful at first.

Four

THE MOMENT SUSAN HEADS UP THE STILL-WHITE DRIVEWAY, she knows something is wrong; it has to be. She couldn't have been stupid enough to leave the kitchen door wide open. Her heart jabs in her throat as she breaks into a run. "Christopher? *Christopher?*" No answer but the sound of her bootsteps on the cold snow, tiny stones dropping onto glass.

Maybe the wind blew the door; maybe she was careless in her haste to escape.

The kitchen is empty; the living room, too, the mohair blanket tossed in a heap behind Christopher's chair. His clothes are gone.

She heads upstairs. Maybe he's taken refuge in their bed or in the closet where his day began. She opens and closes doors, calling, searching. It is not a large house, not like the old one that Christopher built. She looks under their bed; she checks closets, the laundry hamper, the space beneath the bathroom sink. Places he can't possibly fit, small as he is. "Christopher!" Down the hall from their bedroom is a guest room, still piled with boxes she hasn't had time to unpack in the six months they've lived here. "Christopher?"

The room is dark, the shades drawn. The last person who stayed here was Peter, on his way to Gabon for a field biology expedition. Through a narrow aisle between the boxes, she glimpses the neatly made bed, a twin with a navy comforter, a white pillow. Empty. Unused. No sign that Christopher's been there, that he's been back at all.

Then she thinks of the basement. Did she remember to lock that door? She can feel her pulse beat in her throat.

"Christopher?" she calls, flicking on the light at the top of the basement stairs. The stairwell seems to deaden the sound of her voice. "Christopher? You down here?"

The stairs shake as she descends. It would be a miracle for Christopher to make it down the rickety stairs in one piece; the disease makes a flight of stairs look like one flat plane—he would drop through and disappear. "Chris?"

The basement is long and narrow, lit by a single, shadeless bulb that brings to mind an arena for interrogation. To the left of the stairs, the washer and dryer; to the right, nothing but an old broom, a plastic bucket, and an empty kitty litter pan the former owner left behind. At the far end, the water heater; the furnace. Slab floor, concrete block walls. "Chris?" she calls out weakly, though it is clear no one else is here.

She still has her coat on, her boots, and now she grabs Christopher's loden from the hook on the door and turns to sweep the row of amber vials, Christopher's pills, off the kitchen counter and into her pocket where they rattle like candy. If he is not here and his clothes are gone, then chances are that Christopher dressed himself. Ordinarily this might have been cause for a little whoop of celebration, a flush of pride, now it is cause for alarm.

She is leaning across the windshield to brush off the snow when she notices the tracks, veering off from the edge of the driveway as though the walker might have stepped off to avoid bumping into the parked car. Skirting the hood, she bends close to examine what looks like sneaker tread preserved in crispy wafers of compressed snow. Christopher's sneakers? How did he get them on by himself? No matter. The tracks trace a shallow arc across the lawn and down to the road. And there they stop. No matter how deeply she bends to survey the surface of the winter road, she can see nothing but marbled gray and white tire tracks, sprinkled with rock salt.

He hadn't turned the way she had, she thinks. Or she would have seen him on her way back to the house. She straightens. In the other direction, the direction of town, the road is empty.

Gripping the steering wheel, Susan squints against the glare of winter sun that bounces off the arched windows of the brick facades on Main Street. On either curb, the wrought-iron lamps are still draped in dark tangles of juniper and spruce, tied up with red ribbon bows. Tinsel cords, suspending tinsel bells lace them together.

Christopher's wandering started when they moved to this place. He is a box turtle, willing to travel one hundred deliberate miles to get back to his home, wherever home is. Not here. This is her fault, she thinks. She's the one who decided to leave their old house, their old town for this one. A colossal mistake, she's been gradually realizing. A shattering one. Too late to remedy.

But for some time Christopher had not seemed to enjoy their friends' company. Though he acted as though he understood what they were discussing, he remained silent, only getting up to offer the olives around, the cheese plate. Then he settled again, sipping his wine and watching. After one party, Christopher wept, "Your friends don't like me! They think I'm stupid." Not true, she had told him, they love you. They're your friends, too. But was that true? Her friends, his friends, noticing that Christopher was failing, had begun to avoid him.

Halfway down the street, bells begin to chime nine o'clock. Oh God. She half expects to see Christopher dart into the street. The noise of the bells always confuses him. Even with the car windows rolled up, he cowers at the onslaught of cascading chords, of unending hymns. But no, the street ahead is empty.

Susan cuts into the parking space in front of the Cup, the café she and Christopher often go to. To her relief, the young man they like, Jonah, is standing behind the counter. He reminds her a little of their son, Peter, with his long frame, his wiry wrists. And when she arrives with Christopher, he always has a kind smile, a warm greeting that makes her feel as though he cares.

"Cold enough for you?" Jonah asks as she steps up to the counter.

"I'm looking for Christopher," she says, striving to keep her voice steady, reminding herself that panic isn't useful. "You haven't, by any miracle, seen him?"

He shakes his head. "He's missing?"

"Sort of. Gave me the slip a short time ago. I know he comes here sometimes."

Jonah frowns. "Sorry. Want me to call you if I see him?"

"Yes, please." She's surprised to find that Jonah's kindness has brought up tears.

"When I go on break, I'll tell the next person you're looking for him."

Susan nods, picking up the pen beside the register and the clean napkin he offers her. "So if you do see him—" Susan scribbles as she speaks. "My cell, home, the police."

"Hey, I know you and your husband by sight—"

Susan looks up at the young man, his mouth bent in apology. "I'm sorry—I'm Susan—Hunsinger. My husband's Christopher. But he doesn't always know it." Susan hands the napkin back to him. She imagines it getting crumpled, spilled on, falling to the floor in a matter of minutes, but Jonah lifts the tip jar and slips it under, anchored, safe.

Susan tucks a dollar in. "Thanks."

Back on the sidewalk, Susan breathes deeply. The air, though dry, is cold, sharply cold, the kind of cold that makes you feel that every breath might cut you.

"Not to panic," Susan says aloud. "It hasn't been that long." How long? Twenty minutes? Thirty? She wishes she could splinter herself into multiple searchers; she wishes she could call someone to help her look as she might have back home.

Remember, she tells herself, you've always found him. He stands out, particularly here. A few months ago, the gas station owner's wife discovered him and drove him home. A week or so later, the neighbor called to tell her Christopher was in his shed. He's wearing an identification bracelet with her phone number and a tag for medical alert. As soon as he's spotted, she tells herself, someone will call.

Susan slams the car door shut, calling out Christopher's name as she hurries up the side path to the open kitchen door. She left the door open on purpose this time, thinking that if Christopher came back he might find his way in more easily.

But this has never been his house. Why would he recognize it? She barely recognizes it herself. The dead whiteness of it, the horrible washed out trim. So different than the house they used to live in, Christopher's beautiful design. What was the madness that had overtaken her thinking, the distortion that made her believe that Christopher would function better if he wasn't surrounded by reminders of what he'd lost, that she would function better if they started their lives anew. If he'd been lucid, he would have killed her. Perhaps that's what he's doing.

FIVE

JEFF'S OFFICE HAS THREE SIGNS STACKED ON THE DOOR LIKE tiers of a wedding cake: JUVENILE FIRE INSPECTOR; CONSERVATION OFFICER, DEC; JEFF HERDMAN, MSW. His office is a fluorescent cubicle off the concrete corridor that divides the police station from the firehouse. A rabbit warren of offices all tucked in a building that went up after Urban Renewal pulled everything down.

Jeff wasn't around when it happened—he'd been in Vietnam—but sometimes as he walks into the "new" building, faced with corrugated tin and portholes for windows, he feels as though it is somehow his fault that all the beautiful old buildings are gone. Like the greedy had been lying in wait, bent on destroying his town as soon as he left it. As soon as he abandoned his post.

Stupid, grandiose thought. But he can't shake it.

The recruiting office had been in one of the razed buildings. *The price you pay to live free.* He bought that and other stuff. Eighteen. Innocent in certain ways. At the physical, he took one look at the doctor and thought, *I'm sunk.* The doctor had his chart in a folder, was ruminating over it like a textbook. The illness of course intrigued him. It intrigued all doctors. He was used to this.

"Do you feel any pain?" the doctor asked. He was an army doctor. Not someone Jeff knew from home.

He shook his head.

"In your joints, I mean. Your knees."

His knees burned some mornings, like they do this morning, as though they were on fire, but he shook his head. A bone doctor had explained to him once how the bones were calcifying. Some days he was all locked up, like a stuck telescope, his leg fully extended.

"Doesn't bother me. Except when it's really cold."

The doctor looked at him a second. "Shouldn't be a problem over there," he said.

(*Over there*, Jeff remembers. No one ever named the place.)

"Still, with a history like this we could keep you Stateside. Nice warm base in Texas."

He could stay Stateside, pushing papers or peeling potatoes in some desert of a base.

"No, sir. I want to serve." And then he added (it shames him to remember his boy self even now), "*Please.*"

Balancing the cardboard carrier on his palm as though he is a butler with a tray, he gently twists the coffee out of its socket and places it on the corner of Stephanie's desk. She reaches for it without looking up, then withdraws her fingers, wagging them. "Hot, hot, hot," she says, and then, teasingly, when he doesn't stop, "My doughnut?"

"Shit. I'm sorry, Steffie." How'd he forget the doughnuts? He always gets doughnuts: chocolate glaze for Stephanie; powdered cinnamon for Marcia. He can't eat them anymore himself. Doctor's orders. But he is always amazed at the pleasure on the girls' faces as they open their waxy white bags—as though they've been tipped off about diamonds inside, engagement settings, perfect love.

"Forget it," Stephanie says. She, and everyone else, knows what happened earlier this morning. The radio is a leaky bucket. Any info you pour in trickles through the rest of the department and beyond, far beyond. Doesn't help to think about it. He knows he can expect to be treated brusquely by some, tenderly by others. Maybe stood for a beer at lunch or allowed extra minutes on his break to get his wits together in a bathroom stall.

Jeff enters his cubicle, grateful for his privacy. He slips off his winter coat, and then he sits down at his desk, turns on his computer. He needs to talk to Wiltsie. He needs Wiltsie's version of last night, even though he dreads it. Wiltsie doesn't mince words.

On the screen is a long list of e-mails in boldface type. Disaster after disaster he's supposed to attend to from a fire investigation at Drago Tires to a juvenile fire starter at Hillcrest Home. Scrolling the list, he aches to mouth something, a doughnut, a whole box of doughnuts. He'd mash each one to a pulpy wad against his upper pallet, chewing and swallowing until the world disappeared.

Wiltsie raps the side of the cubicle. "How's it going?"

"Got a minute?"

Wiltsie, in his civvies, black wool slacks and a plaid flannel shirt, is on his way home from the night shift, but with a bare nod, he hitches his pant leg and plants his shoe on the empty chair like he's waiting for a shine.

Jeff swings round to face him. "Leanne finally showed up."

"Bitch. What'd she tell you?"

"Not much."

Wiltsie rubs a hand over his knee, plucking a bit of lint. "Caught her up to Rydell's place like you said."

Jeff nods, trying to keep his expression neutral. One flinch will blow it.

"Not a pretty sight, my friend. Got my light shining in her eyes, so she's blinder than a bat. Still she wants to fight me."

"Jimmy?"

"Can't tell what the hell or who the hell's under that blanket. Leanne doesn't seem to care. She's shouting about warrant this, warrant that, and I tell her, 'Hold up. Someone was concerned.'" Wiltsie snorts. "Your woman didn't like that."

Jeff watches Wiltsie remove his foot from the chair. He's a strange guy. Lives with his mother in an apartment above the bank and moonlights as a maître d'. But Jeff trusts him. He knows how to keep his mouth shut.

"You don't want me saying this, but I'm saying it anyhow. Time to take out the trash, pal."

Six

Jeff is not a good sleeper. Years of being awakened by late-night calls, years of his brittle rest snapped in all the wrong places, until there was no right place. If he did sleep, he dreamt dreams worth being woken from—even for the nightmares he is summoned to. Dreams of There. He doesn't like to talk about it.

A year ago, Leanne bought them a bed filled with water that rolled when you rolled and gurgled from time to time like a contented baby. The plastic lining always felt clammy, and whenever he moved in it, he sank, but Jeff didn't like to complain. Her buying an expensive bed meant that he meant something to his wife, he thought. It meant Leanne planned to stay.

She said the bed made her feel safe, like a baby snugged between her mama's thighs. He was certain *her* mama had never held her that way, but did not say this. He had no experience with babies except the ones always splattered with something, always dragging their diapers, their mothers tagging behind, looking for places to sink themselves.

Once seated, those mothers let their babies loose, lit their cigarettes, free at last to exhale their exhaustion. He'd been raised this way. He can see his mother even now, leaning against the screen door of the farmhouse, her hips rising as though to meet a lover's, a veil of smoke shielding her from the mess of toys and neighbor children scattered before her in the dusty yard.

Last week he had listened as a young mother stood in the door of her double-wide, told her story beginning to end in a voice as dead as an andiron. The five kids; the boyfriend with the video camera; the locked cabinet she didn't even know was there. Behind her the kids were listening, wondering who the stranger was, where they were going next. She didn't mention the drugs the police had found, the fire in the shed that he was there to investigate. And when she called the children, they scattered like mice from the carving knife.

He told Leanne the bed made him queasy. That was just him, she said. He made himself queasy. He made her queasy, too.

He did not tell her about the dreams he'd had in that bed. Dreams of drowning, though he worked with fire. Black-suited divers, crouched on the banks of a swollen river like black rocks, readying themselves to tumble into the lane of iron water, toward the pair of flailing arms.

This morning he'd turned once, expecting his shoulder to find hers, expecting his hip to touch hers as he rolled himself to face her. In the small breadth of waking, he'd had a thought: a trip to Disney. One of those package deals. A condo with a concrete balcony overlooking a paradise of too many activities to choose from. He grinned like a fool, like a man who had found the answer to all of life's ills. She'll like this idea. She might even make love to him for his thoughtfulness.

That his perfect vacation was hours of fishing at a quiet hole, hours and hours of utter silence, was not important. In the penumbra of joy and lust he suddenly inhabited, it didn't matter to Jeff what he liked.

"Leanne?"

His left elbow sank into the plastic sheath, putting stress on his aching rotator, so that he buckled, flopping forward on his own face. And that's when the memory of the night cascaded over him. The several wakings. The liquid green numbers of the clock: 2:35; 4:30; 5:00. The night almost pure black outside.

He didn't bother with a robe. Just pulled on his jacket slung across the chair, his jeans and winter boots. For years he'd been a man with a set of clothes at the ready.

A hard black morning. Stars still out. He rooted around the yard. For what? His truck was there on the gravel; her Toyota was not.

He knew who she was with. Jimmy D. She'd been flirting with Jimmy D. for months. Last night at Earl's, she sat way down the bar, pretending like she wasn't with her husband. Silly girly stuff. Showing off. A shaker tilted on a bed of salt. A teaspoon plastered to the end of her nose. Leanne and the boy knew it was silly. That was half the fun. Acting like you were a kid and didn't care. She was a kid compared with him, her husband. He was almost fifty. But Jimmy D. Jimmy D. must be eighteen. No more than that. He had a fence of pimples across his brow and a milkiness to his skin. He was narrow hipped and his arms and legs dangled. Leanne was twenty-five. She ought to know better, but of course she didn't.

He'd ignored them. Or played at it. He sat at his end of the bar, nursing a beer, appearing to be lost in his own thoughts, but actually straining to hear their chatter, to monitor its intensity under the din of the jukebox and the hockey game on the floating TV. He knew he wasn't fooling anybody. Mo Sanders came up to him after a while, flicking his eyes to the pair down the bar as he passed them. *What's it to you?* Jeff wanted to say, but didn't. Mo's wife, Doreen, weighed close to three hundred pounds, made chitchat all day long at the diner where she waitressed, but no one would call *her* a flirt.

Jeff turned back to the house. He'd watched them leaving the bar together, Jimmy D.'s long, thin arm draped over Leanne's shoulders, snugging her to him. He could have gotten up then. He could have cocked a fist and threatened Jimmy to settle it outside. So why didn't he? He was scared. Not of Jimmy. That kid would go down with one well-aimed punch. No. He was scared of Leanne. Scared of losing her. He could kick himself a million times, but that's how he saw it. Give Leanne her freedom and he had a chance. Try to restrain her and she'd snap back so fast she'd break the shank.

Where would they have gone? Jimmy D.'s, of course. He worked the Rydell place over to Milton. Rydell, cheap as a goat, milked sixty head, went through farm help like Dixie cups, and the shed where the help lived was a firetrap. Jeff had inspected it for the squad last year. Seventy violations in all, including outdated wiring and a load too heavy for the voltage. When he'd handed Rydell his Christmas list, the old farmer spat on it and shoved it in Jeff's breast pocket.

The worry grew sharper, poked into him, his gut, right side. The truth is, he was more worried about what might have happened to her, plastered and reckless as she was, than that she was cheating.

Hell, what he'd seen. Drunks wrapped around trees, hanging upside down by their shoulder straps. If they were lucky. But more often he saw their bodies rocketed through the windshield. Bodies, snapped at the neck, experiencing a flexibility they never knew in life.

He reached for the telephone. *Stop imagining,* Wiltsie will say, *you're not the first guy on the planet whose wife's gone bed hopping. Not the first or the last.* But he can't stop. The shit-faced fools were smoking in bed. The match flying God-knows-where, the still-lit butts embedding themselves in the cotton-batted mattress. Floating them to hell on a raft of flames.

When Wiltsie answered, Jeff took a deep breath and felt like a wave backed up in his chest. "Find Leanne," he said. "Rydell's bunkhouse. But make it anonymous, Wiltsie. Please."

Half an hour later, Jeff heard the car doors slam, whack and whack, one after the other, throaty and sure. Followed by the sound of gravel spitting underfoot and a curse trumpeted into the dawn.

"Motherfucker, motherfucking pussy!"

He held his body stiff, imagining what it would be like to be dead, dead of sorrow, dead of pain. He used to lie like this as a boy, willing himself dead while he listened to his mother and her boyfriend go at it through the walls.

"Get out here, fucker!"

Leanne was shouting, waking the neighbor dogs who howled with her as though they'd been summoned. Her rage reminded him of the final roar of a backdraft that explodes through the roof, shooting toward the sky. Parking lots, the fire crew called them. Nothing left standing in the end.

Then, contradicting her own words, Leanne crashed through the front door, through the kitchen, and into the bedroom.

He rolled, flicked on the light. She was striding toward him. Her hair loose and electric, a shade of red people would swear was dyed but was not. And he wondered if she was going to jump him, which he'd welcome, of course. He'd welcome her arms vised around him, her thighs girding his.

She read his mind and stayed put. "Fucker," she said. The word shoved at him, shoved all the way into him, like a hoof. Then her voice squeaked an imitation, " 'Investigating a break-in.' Like I don't know what the fuck you and Wiltsie are up to?"

Behind her, Jimmy D. pinned his gangly frame to the doorway, looking on the scene with no apology and no fear, just like a boy who was nearly dead from fatigue and possibly drunk enough to vomit.

But Leanne wasn't done. "Get out of *my* bed. Get out of *my* house!" She rushed to the end of the bed. Ripping out the bottom sheet, she tried rolling him out.

Jeff straightened his legs, froze his torso like a corpse, a dead-weight against her effort to tip him onto the floor. A small part of him was enjoying this, was flung back to feeling like a small boy in a hammock, rocked or swung by bigger boys. He remembered bracing and swaying almost exactly like this, clinging to the sides of the hammock like a bat so they couldn't dump him.

Leanne was growing frustrated and Jimmy D. wasn't lifting a finger to help.

"Bastard," she said.

"Me or him?"

To his surprise, this seemed to deflate her. She sat on the edge of the bed, and she could have been a mother seated there to tuck in her child, except that her nostrils flared like tiny agitated wings and her breath flowed over him hot and beery.

"Oh fuck you," she said. She stood and moved to the doorway, snagging Jimmy's arm and pulling him after her as she left the house.

SEVEN

"PICK UP, LINE THREE. JEFF HERDMAN. LINE THREE."

In the bathroom, Jeff bunches and tosses a paper towel and ignores the miss in his haste to get back to his cubicle. Line three is reserved for search-and-rescue calls; line four, for fire inspection. When he returned from the war, he thought he'd try dairy farming, but he didn't have any relatives who still farmed or enough money to buy his own place. Instead he went back to school on the GI Bill, got his degree in social work, volunteered at the local fire department, and trained to be an investigator. It was as though, after being in Vietnam, he couldn't function without a stream of adrenaline coursing through him. It was an addiction, the way some people needed caffeine to jangle themselves awake. So after all that, he started taking civil service tests, finally got a job with the Department of Environmental Conservation, and part of that training certified him in search and rescue and EMT.

He needed crisis, or the possibility of one. He needed to be in the thick of it, though he often thought he'd be better off spending a hundred dull hours a week plowing a field.

Then the joint problems worsened; he'd had to go on disability. Eventually, he'd carved a niche. Fire and rescue and safety. It was still the center of all things. It still stirred him. He was content.

Sliding into his chair, he punches down the flashing button, picks up the receiver as he positions his assignment pad to the middle of the blotter. "Hel-lo. Jeff Herdman speaking."

It's Higgs on the line. Lieutenant Higgs. Sounding every bit like his pompous self.

"What's up, Lieutenant?"

"Missing person. A walkaway. White, male, elderly."

"The home?"

"Fourteen-oh-one Hillside Drive. Wife reported it. Dementia's a factor."

"Time?"

Higgs pauses. "Call came in ten-thirty. Wife estimates he took off about nine this morning. She's been out looking ever since. Says she covered downtown, the Cup, the library, places he might find on his own."

It was ten-fifty now. What has Higgs been doing? Washing his underwear? "What's the temperature?"

"Ten."

Jeff sighs. "History?"

"In the past, spouse recovered without assistance."

A bastard search. Named for what the searchers called the guy when he was found snug and comfy in his tent. "Where?"

Higgs clears his throat. "Didn't ask."

"Name?"

"Christopher Hunsinger; wife, Susan. Downstaters. Been up about nine months."

"The wife's home?"

"Yeah."

"Best get moving, Higgs. I'll meet you there." With luck they might find the bastard.

Ten minutes later, Jeff pulls slowly into a wide, snow-slicked driveway that leads to a small white Cape set primly on a rise. Off to the right, Higgs is lounging trooper-style against the side of his patrol car as if this day were made for sunning.

Jeff looses a low whistle as Higgs raises a gloved hand. He's a tall man; lean; face frozen behind the dark glasses, the stiff collar.

"Great day for wheelies." Jeff thumps the trunk of the patrol car. "Department won't spring for snow tires?"

Higgs shrugs. "Patch of ice."

"Shame." Fuck Higgs and his carelessness. He's cut onto the lawn, leaving an arc of scaly tread on the otherwise unbroken surface of snow, a perfect medium for recording tracks until the sun grows too warm or the wind begins to blow.

"Get in," Higgs says.

The air inside the car is close and smells faintly of the soapy aftershave the police seem to like. He borrowed some once after a shift at the firehouse, and Leanne made him scrub it off before she'd let him kiss her.

"All right," Higgs says, turning down the volume on his radio. "Tarlow's sending enough men right off to deploy some grids—"

"Whoa, whoa, whoa."

Higgs's glasses are off, and Jeff can see his eyes narrow and the worm of a muscle squirm once in the hollow of his cheek.

"Got a problem, Herdman?"

"By the time you get that bunch of assholes assembled and organized, the old man's going to have frozen to death." What he wants to do is run a hasty—ten highly trained searchers who have free rein to make their own judgments, who work fast, who know how to look for clues, footprints and broken branches, a fleck of color, a patch of urine, a thorn apple or a blackberry bramble laden with human hair. Managing a search is a balance of probability of detection and search time. Probability of detection is based on the skill of the rescuers and the search area. In this case, the rescuers are not skilled.

Higgs's tie knot rises and falls beneath his Adam's apple and for a moment it looks like Jeff's gotten to him. "Fuck you, Herdman." Higgs cracks open his door, readies to step out.

"Hold it," Jeff says. "What'd she say the point-last-seen was?"

Higgs pulls in his foot. "Living room."

"You mean there?" Jeff points to a matched set of windows framed by white café curtains.

Higgs squints. "Probably."

"Now look—" Framed by the windshield, a set of footprints embedded in the snow slides away under the front of the car. "Open your door again."

Higgs stares at the sliver of ground. "Shit. How do I get out?"

Jeff grins. "Carefully."

He needs his camera, which is stowed in his ready bag in the office, which he did not bring. Judging from the pain in his intestines, he had known that this wasn't a day he could take to the field. He'll be lucky to pull off puttering around the house, building a rapport with the wife, acting as liaison with base command.

He should wait for the others before starting the search. But here he is with fresh track in front of him. Truth is, he doesn't have his trained search team, his hasty, even if he had the go-ahead. Luke and Dan, the only other properly trained searchers in the county, have headed out of state for the weekend, worthy causes like a wedding and a funeral. Just a holler and they would be here for him, but how many marriages can he ruin like his own? They wouldn't make it back in time anyway.

The track is perfect, the fresh, cold snow holds the mold of the man's shoes like a fossil, which Jeff is 99 percent sure, hunkered down as he is and peering at the backward vees of the impression, are sneakers, Nikes, low topped, well worn (note how the depth of the impression deepens—the man walks on his heels—but the tread lightens). And he can tell that both shoelaces are already untied or were never tied, which means the feet might work their way out of the low-topped sneaker after a certain amount of time, depending on the walker's pace, the snugness of the shoes, and whether or not he's wearing socks.

If he had his ready bag like he ought to, he'd get out his tape measure and lay it down to check the length of the stride and the width of the straddle. From those measurements alone, he could tell if the man is bowlegged, if his balls ache, if he is wandering lost or has a destination in mind.

Jeff drops to his belly, stretches his arm along the edge of the track as a gauge. Christopher Hunsinger is short strided like himself, shoulder to fingertip, heel to heel, except where he breaks a stride, pigeoning left, overstriding right, which tells Jeff that even on the flat hard surface of the frozen lawn there are obstacles for Christopher, obstacles in his mind, but also a destination.

If a man is lost, his dominant foot will point along the line he takes. And pitch angles will vary foot to foot. The dominant foot takes a slightly longer step than the nondominant foot. Think about it, he will later instruct the man's wife. A blind man walking across a flat plain will follow a large circle toward his nondominant foot. The dominant calf muscles can lift more weight, stride longer, farther. We circle our weak side, wheeling, wheeling, and never even realize we're doing so.

But here is evidence that Christopher is fighting against his dominance, like a rower pushing hard against the rim of the tide. A hitch here, a stumble there. Then a sharp turn onto the road. Squatting, Jeff surveys the road's surface, a slurry of salt and tire sludge, the deep grime of winter travel, not a surface for recording tracks.

"Are you coming?" It's Higgs calling from the driveway.

Jeff raises his hand to silence him, not bothering to turn around. *Where are you headed, Christopher? Where did you need to go?* These aren't the tracks of a lost man. Not yet.

On the other side of the road, a new forest springs up beyond the drainage ditch—white pine and aspen and black cherry and locust, a deep screen that should shunt the old man up or down the road. If the volunteers arrive soon enough, there's a chance they can sweep him back along the road as though he were that one wandering, stupid ram who breaks through the wire fence to nibble the world beyond. Everything Jeff's been taught says don't waste your time on the densely grown side, particularly if the person is disoriented, so he turns up the road, checking the ditch as he breaks into a jog. With any luck, Christopher stepped onto its porcelain lip, slipped into its basin, and lies beached, waiting for someone to rescue him.

EIGHT

A SHORT WALKWAY OF SLATE SQUARES CUTS FROM THE TOP OF the driveway to the front door, yet hardly anyone ever enters the house that way. The country yard is too long and wide for a path leading from the road to the front door, and besides, there's nowhere to park, really. Not much shoulder along the rail fence that marks the border of the property on that side.

Yet someone is knocking on the front door, and before Susan can reach it the doorbell is ringing two syrupy notes. Outside on the stair, two men stand side by side, a policeman in a dark navy uniform and a much smaller man in mustard-colored jeans and a down coat.

The policeman touches his cap. "Susan Hunsinger?"

"Thank God you're here."

"Lieutenant Higgs. We spoke on the telephone."

"Hello," she says, shaking his hand with a firmness that seems to surprise him. "And you?" She turns to the smaller man.

"Jeff Herdman. I'm out of DEC. I'll be Incident Command."

They, too, shake hands. She peers at him. Such a small man must be used to being mistaken for a sidekick, she thinks. "Come in, please. We can sit right here in the living room."

The men's radios squawk quietly on their belts as they cross the room to the sofa. Susan follows them, still talking, though she thinks, perhaps, she should be quiet. "Thanks for getting here so quickly. Both of you. I should have called sooner, but I thought I could find him on my own. First I looked in the usual places, then I came home and tried to follow his tracks—"

She seats herself on the ladder-back chair opposite the men. Between them is the coffee table she'd pushed aside earlier to clear space for her yoga.

"You saw the tracks?"

It's the small man. He's leaning forward intently, as though he might hear something beyond her speech.

"On the front lawn, running almost parallel to the driveway. I found them, and I lost them quite quickly. As soon as they reached the road."

Jeff heaves a light cough into his fist. "I saw them, too. Tough to follow once you hit the road."

"I hope I didn't screw anything up. That would be like me."

Lieutenant Higgs shifts his shoulders. "Best thing is call us right away."

Susan nods, feeling the heat rise in her cheekbones. "In the future, it's a deal. Now where do we begin?"

"We'll start with this form," Jeff says, tapping the clipboard on his lap with his ballpoint pen. "A few questions to get us all on the same page."

"Okay," Susan says. "But let's do this quickly. It's freezing out there." And every second, Christopher is possibly moving farther and farther away, uncharted, unaccounted for, untethered in what seems a square mile the size of the universe. Then, judging from the men's expressions, she amends herself, "I'm sorry. I don't mean to be rude."

Jeff smiles. "No problem, Mrs. Hunsinger"—*Doctor* Hunsinger, she corrects inside her head—"but we can't ask our guys to just look for a person, any person."

"I'm sorry. Ask me your questions. I just want to find him."

"We all do." Seated beside tall Higgs, Jeff looks even smaller than he did on the stair, a manikin with a boy's narrow hips, a man's muscled shoulders evident even beneath his puffy down coat. Christopher is small like this. All his life, he's had to calibrate his manner to counter the impression of his size.

Jeff clears his throat. "We need a physical description, Mrs. Hunsinger—"

"Doctor." There it is, she can't contain herself.

Jeff blinks. "*Doctor* Hunsinger. Great, that's what I mean, detail. Let's start with height."

"Five feet eight inches; weight, a hundred eighty-five—medium build; left-handed; Caucasian; white hair—whorled—"

"Okay. Slow down."

Susan watches him jot her answers on the form. He, too, is left-handed.

"Facial hair?"

"No. None. Clean shaven. High cheekbones—" She breaks off. "This is silly of me. I have a photograph. Right here." She draws the newspaper clipping from her handbag on the floor.

"Recent?"

"Recent enough." Susan knows why Higgs asks. The photograph makes Christopher look like an astronaut or an actor. The keen eyes, the rakish smile. An air of perpetual good health.

It had appeared in the local newspaper just before they left their town. "Local Architect Christopher Hunsinger and Scientist Wife, Susan, Leaving University for Greener Pastures" read the caption.

"Any dementia?"

"He's disoriented most of the time. But he vacillates. Even

last week there was a moment—" As though a needle had dipped down, found its groove. "He looked at me and said, 'I think I'm not thinking anymore.' Then back to gibberish." Back to sentences knotted up in his cortex, tripping him. And her. "It was bizarre."

"He's wandered before?"

Susan nods. "Several times."

Higgs turns to Jeff. "Previously recovered in town."

"I've checked the Cup, the gas station, the library." She can hear her voice rising, a thin tangle in her throat.

"In the past, did he ever find his way home?" Jeff leans toward her as he asks this. His tone professionally softened.

"In the past, I found him. Which is why I delayed." Heat grips her throat and she glances down at the pine-needle-flecked carpet.

"I'm sure you did your best, Dr. Hunsinger," Jeff says. He checks his wristwatch and cuts a look at Higgs. *He thinks I'm an idiot,* Susan thinks. *Or an egomaniac.* "It's been an hour and forty-five minutes."

"That long?" The pulse has started again in her neck. She counsels herself to breathe.

"Let's go to what your husband is wearing. Footwear?"

"Sneakers, I think."

"Brand?" Jeff is scribbling and nodding as though she is finally saying something important.

"Nike," she says. "The only ones he can get on by himself."

"Socks?"

Susan hesitates. "White cotton ankle socks, I think, but whether they stayed on—frankly, I don't know exactly what he's wearing. He was wearing a flannel pajama shirt when I last saw him—he was sleeping, and I laid out a pair of tan slacks next to him, black boxers—" Susan is aware that both men are staring at her. "It was a complicated morning. Started off fine, then deteriorated. I don't know if either one of you has experience—" The men shake their heads in tandem. "By the time I got him calmed down enough to fall asleep, I had to get a break, a quick walk, to check the mail, and when I came back—"

"Okay," Jeff says, nodding. "I'm getting more of the picture."

Susan blinks, presses her middle finger to the ridge between her eyebrows. "A pretty crappy one." And it's her fault, isn't it? If she hadn't been so indulgent, if she'd just stayed inside?

"Yeah."

"Outerwear, ma'am?" Higgs interrupts.

Susan can see from the look on Jeff's face he isn't pleased.

"His London Fog's gone. His winter coat's still here. I checked the downstairs closet carefully, and that's the coat I think is definitely missing."

"Color? Style?" Jeff has the reins again.

"Tan trench, raglan sleeves, slit pockets. A simple collar."

Jeff flashes a smile at her. "Good job. You'd be surprised how few people can remember their own coats in a situation like this. Let alone someone else's."

"I'm a scientist," Susan says. Even as she says this, she thinks, *So what, lady.*

"What kind?" Jeff asks, sounding genuinely interested.

"Microbiologist. I'm a professor." Self-centered spout, she scolds herself.

"Your husband's a doctor, too?"

"An architect."

Jeff nods. "Children?"

"One son who's out of the country. In Africa. Gabon."

Jeff cocks an eyebrow. "I'm guessing you're not from around here."

"We moved at the end of August."

"Jewelry?"

"ID bracelet—unless it slipped off. And his wedding ring. Two strands, twisted, silver and gold."

Jeff frowns. "Meds?"

"Nitro patch; Prozac; Lipitor; glyburide—Micronase, 2.5 milligrams. I managed to give it to him this morning, but he took off before I could feed him anything. Do you know what that means?" Confusion. Dizziness. Possible stroke.

Jeff's gaze meets hers. "I'm a licensed EMT, but we don't need to go there yet. It hasn't been that long."

"But you'll make a note."

"Of course. And missed dosage Prozac, Lipitor," Jeff intones as he scribbles his notes. "You were able to patch him?"

Susan nods. That part was easy. A dot to his chest. He never even noticed.

"Anything else? Other than that he's in good shape?"

"Great shape," she says.

Jeff glances at his watch again. "Estimate three quarters of an hour from call-in; hour and forty-five from PLS."

"What's that?"

"Point-last-seen," Higgs says.

"Okay," Susan says. "I'm confused. Who are you?"

Jeff leans toward Susan. "It's all right. It is confusing. This is a small town, so I've got to wear a few hats. Lieutenant Higgs here, he'll be coordinating the police, the fire people, and the volunteers. Me, I'm the only certified search-and-rescue person in the area, so I'll be the liaison between base and you."

"If you're the professional, why won't you be searching?"

Jeff sighs. "I'd sure like to, but I've got some health issues. Don't worry, though. We'll do whatever's necessary to find your husband."

"'Whatever's necessary.' What does that mean exactly?"

National Guard? SWAT? A small town can't possibly have a lot of resources. If she were still in Princeton, so many people she could call—but that's not helpful, not useful. She's got her own resources. She's got her brain. "I'm going to need maps," she says. "Topographical; geological survey; tax, county—"

Jeff slips his pen beneath the clipboard clasp, then looks up at her. "We'll bring you into this as soon as we can, Doctor. Right now it's a matter of getting organized."

"I want to do something now."

"You want to help?" Lieutenant Higgs stands up.

Susan nods.

"Sit tight," he says.

NINE

From the window in the living room, Susan watches the volunteers arriving. The milling, stomping, heavy-breathing men dressed head to foot in mustard-colored jumpsuits and boots and ski masks remind her of a herd of steaming cattle. A peculiar boiling energy seems to fill them as they climb out of truck cabs and low-riding cars, hustling, despite bulky clothes, to the tent the police have constructed on the front lawn. Shouted greetings, braying laughter. With all these pickups parked in front, she worries that Christopher will not recognize the driveway or his house or even the stretch of road on which the house stands. What can she do? Where can they go? The worry, she tells herself, is irrational. Christopher will be seen before he sees, she tells herself. They will find him and bring him home.

Dr. Hunsinger is a stoic—Jeff can tell. It's not just the way she looks—late middle-aged, straight and slim, with smooth white hair that swings like a silky fabric when she turns her head, and blue, opalescent eyes—it's the way she holds herself. She reminds him of a woman in an advertisement. Not the kind of middle-aged lady you see in real life. Not like his mother, who, last seen, was about fifty pounds overweight and wearing polyester stretch pants and a caftan plastered with green fronds.

And Susan Hunsinger is also seriously smart. Now she is sitting at the kitchen table, studying the maps that he left behind while he went to check on operations, scribbling notes on a pad as though she is planning the day's search, as though her intellect and her intuition might bring some clarity to the picture.

A woman bent over her cards, Jeff thinks as he walks back into the kitchen. His mother used to read the cards, straining to divine the undivinable from a row of contorted faces. His only game is solitaire. A loneliness peopled by a royal court.

"What're you finding?" he asks. He's already outlined the plan in his mind.

Susan looks up, fixing him with an unsentimental gaze. She has his compass, and she is using it as a protractor—checking plausible bearings, perhaps, plausible routes. "If you're following a hypothesis that Christopher's chosen the path of least resistance, you're going to head up here—" Her finger traces a taupe line, a trail that bumps up latitudes, negotiates longitudes. "But what if—" She closes her eyes and he knows she's imagining herself inside her husband's uneven gait, his frayed mind. Her eyes open again. "Well, where does he go? What propels him forward? Scent? Desire? Fright?" A vision of a place to rest?

"Depends," Jeff says, pulling out the chair beside her, but committing only a knee to its seat as he leans his palm on the table. "Let's see." Looking down at his maps, he feels a certain shyness about his own possessions because it is clear that Susan feels they are her possessions now, such is the confidence with which she taps her index finger on the taupe-colored thread then slides her compass to the spot with the smoothness of a planchette floating over the polished surface of a Ouija board.

Jeff clears his throat. "The ditches have been searched from here to town and back the other direction, north, for a couple of miles. The general rule with walkaways—they walk until they reach a barrier, an obstacle they can't cross or climb over or under. They veer—"

"The woods present too many obstacles—"

"Exactly." She is quick. "Think of the trees as so many posts. Broken limbs, fallen trunks barring the way. We start by searching an open grid across the fields—"

Jeff places a piece of blank graph paper in front of Susan and a ballpoint pen, a white, chewed stick that he draws from his pocket. "It's a grid search," he says. "We start at the edge of the road, spread out about six feet apart. You want your peripheral vision to overlap the guys' on either side—"

Susan watches him place small neat X's in the row of tiny squares, pulling from them parallel lines that slice the page. Why is it that some men like to draw as they think? Christopher did.

"Then we move straight across, no matter what's in front of us. If it's swamp, we go through swamp; if it's brambles, we go through brambles."

The paper now has tangles of blackberry and stands of cattail, Susan notes. No trees. "What keeps you straight?" she asks.

"String."

"String?"

"Twine," Jeff says. "The anchor's unrolling it as he walks. Every ten paces, he ties a ribbon. The kind surveyors use."

"Slow, then," Susan says.

"Very slow." Jeff nods.

"When they find something?"

"The line stops, everyone waits. They bring out the gloves, the evidence bags, the camera."

"Meticulous."

"You better know how to wait."

"And if you don't find anything?" Susan fixes him with a look which he meets with those strange blue eyes.

"We start all over again."

"This is the best way to find Christopher, you think?" She isn't finished with him, Jeff can see. "I think it's time to depart from the general rule. If we look where he might have turned *in*, not *away*, we might see routes. We might. Deer find routes."

"Walkaways don't." The words, the tone, he regrets the instant they are sprung.

She doesn't notice. She's used to being in charge. Navigator and captain both.

"See this?" She taps the map. "Frozen marshes, fire lanes, spaghetti roads, old dumps. Ways into the forest that present no obstacles."

She's right. He has been avoiding this thought, veering, himself, from the more complex logistics of a winter tracking. Complexities he has not yet informed her of. Whether to use dogs eventually. Right now the sun is bright, the temperature extremely cold, the air crisp but still. Not a hint of wind to carry a scent. And the trail—such as it is—will soon be trampled to bits by hordes of firemen, some lugging full turnout gear. He has tried to convince the newbies and the heros that what protects from heat turns deadly in the cold, that they'll freeze from the inside out, that their coats trap the moisture from their sweaty T-shirts against their skin, causing reverse hypothermia.

Forget it. Each guy believes his own truth. Higgs has chosen to deploy grids over further tracking, over Jeff's objections. This is a world in which rank trumps experience. Like in 'Nam.

So you make nice, make nice to everyone. To the lieutenant and to the chief, whose men will set off tally-stepping across the field like the Roman legion. It's 20 degrees at noon, and in an hour, their minds will be dull and their toes and fingers numb, and all they will think about is supper or sex or a place to get warm.

He plans to send the worst ones to the area where they can do the least damage. Let them swagger up and down the empty fields, dreaming of honors to come. Only remember to call them in before they die of boredom and the cold.

Susan's right. There are entrances to the woods. He's seen them, too. There should be a police car at each one of them. A fire truck parked across the break, lights twirling. There should be a track trap, a swath of sand or dirt across the road, across the fire lane, to catch Christopher's prints—he'd have to make it himself, but who would take over? The chief and the lieutenant don't have a clue how to read tracks. There should be a helicopter with forward-looking infrared, a thermal-imaging camera. But the chief says he *don't like rushing to wait for nothing.* Lieutenant Higgs warns, *Who the hell's going to pay?*

Containment means locking down two, three, four, five police vehicles for God knows how long at important points that Christopher might walk by. Which they won't do. Too damn expensive. Maybe for a lost child—or the President of the United States. Not for an old man wandering in the cold.

Jeff tugs at the bill of his cap. "It's early. Christopher might show up yet wanting his soup."

"If he knew how to ask for it," Susan says. "How cold is it now?"

"You don't want to focus on that."

"I do."

"Twenty. Twenty degrees Fahrenheit. No wind."

Susan bites a knuckle. "If he keeps moving, then."

"If he's found a place to warm up."

"Both things are possible."

"Entirely possible. You ever heard of a 'bastard search'?"

"No."

"That's a search where the guys check all the likely places—"

"I did that—"

Jeff holds up his palm to stop her. "Only to find the bastard sitting all comfy back at home."

"I see, the 'bastard' didn't bother to tell anyone he was leaving—"

"Well, you'd be surprised how many times searchers forget to leave a note letting the jerk know they're out looking."

Susan looks at Jeff, who sits across from her at the kitchen table, gently knocking his knuckles on its surface. In the last hour, she has started to trust this man. She cannot put a finger on exactly why. "Decent" is the word that comes to mind. He seems a truly decent man. There is something about his physical self that makes you understand that. The blue-green eyes in the chiseled face, the squared-off chin, and his strange gait, a shuffle followed by a slight hop, like a man straining against stiff knees.

"He likes the cold."

"Yeah?"

"He was stationed in the Arctic with the Corps of Engineers. Loved it. We had a closet filled with gear—government issue—that used to embarrass me on the slopes. He wore this awful felt mask. He looked like a monster, a lunatic, but he didn't care. A tent over the nose, a grille across the mouth. He was happy as a clam. I wish he had it now."

Jeff nods.

"I want to join the search."

"That's not a good idea."

"Why not?"

Jeff dips his chin, straining the back of his neck as he stifles a sigh.

"You think I'd be too emotional."

"No."

"A distraction."

"Something like that."

"I can keep to myself. I'm comfortable in the woods. Out of doors. I studied field biology before I turned to cells. Christopher and I loved to ski. Besides, I'm the one he knows—if he hears my voice—"

"I can advise you, I can't stop you. Who's going to be inside?"

"You."

So she sets off again on foot. By herself. Trudging past the volunteers who are still waiting to be told where to go, chatting, smoking, in the cold air. She feels gazes, but they do not speak. The bolder of the men touch their caps, catch her eye. Glances which she cannot return, concentrating as she is on putting one foot in front of the other, on not slipping on the slick white driveway. Jeff's disapproval is a steady beam at her back, but she's fairly sure he's not following her, that he's given her leave to muck up things as she wishes.

Stick to the road, he told her. The woods are a shield, a barrier, keeping Christopher out, he said, but she disagrees. She keeps thinking of Oedipus at Colonus, the ruined king finding refuge in the grove. Restless, blind Oedipus—she hasn't thought of him since the summer of her senior year when she read the entire trilogy in Greek, the broken man who stumbles the rocky terrain led by his wife—no, his daughter, of course. His wife doesn't lead— she exiles him, slamming the door, washing her hands of his delirium. She cannot, in the end, be counted as one of the faithful.

Across the road, stands of sumac rise in an elegant screen of faded crimson and rust. Susan halts, turns to face up the road, which stretches, a desolate tongue, to nowhere. Come on, Christopher. Show up. She squints into the empty horizon, hoping to conjure his form, to see the trees' markings materialize into coat and pants, the shuffling gait of a cold but determined man returning home.

In the fields to the right, the line of volunteers steps in perfect unison, not Mother, May I, but Mother, I May Not. The light streams down, making diamonds in the snow on the meadow. Fairy dust sifts down from the trees. Susan swings to face back to town. Perhaps Jeff's right. She should sit tight. She should stay inside and let the searchers inform the missing that he is found.

She is standing on the rise up the road, above the house. The very route she trod this morning, breathing lungfuls of relief at getting away. From here, it looks like a party, she thinks. Pickups parked up and down both shoulders and into the driveway. It looks like one of those gatherings you pass on a country road on a summer's day. From your car you glimpse a tent in the yard, a fist of balloons, a silver keg hoisted like a statue on a folding chair, and you wonder what good fortune has befallen that particular family. A graduation. A wedding. A good harvest.

And yet this is the opposite. A community has gathered to solve a crisis.

The tops of her cheeks have lost feeling, her toes, too, and a patch dead center of each of her earlobes, but she cannot leave this spot, the slight rise that gives her a vantage point. She cannot leave Christopher out here alone.

"Dr. Hunsinger!"

It's Jeff, of course. She waves briefly but turns away, lifting her binoculars to her eyes. If she spots Christopher first, lumbering or staggering up or down the road, he will know her. He won't be scared.

Jeff is holding out a knit hat, Day-Glo orange, probably his own. "C'mon now." He puts a hand on her shoulder. "You've got to be cold."

I don't feel anything, she wants to say. But it's not true.

TEN

AT SCHOOL, THEY THOUGHT EVERYTHING WAS HIS FAULT, TOO. He knew this because though he didn't speak, he could hear and he could see. He could see the principal talking to his teacher in the frame of the doorway. Their talk was always sideways, their noses pointed toward each other. But sometimes their looks pointed to him. He could not be accused of causing trouble, he knew, because he caused nothing, nothing at all. But he knew they were discussing his crime and his badness, waiting for his evil to leap out and seize them.

When recess came, he clung to the far fence, trying to keep away, but the boys came after him: *Whatcha gonna torch today? Your balls?* And the girls sang, *Corey Byer, big fat liar, whyn't you set yer ass on fire?* All through recess, their taunts rang and the wood chips they scooped from around the play set flew, stinging his arms, his legs, until the bell rang. No one tried to stop them.

Back in the schoolroom, he knew he would find something in his desk he hadn't put there, something newly dead: a field mouse with shiny eyes; a cluster of black flies curled on their backs; a garter snake; a worm.

He never said anything. Just shoved the corpses back into the recess of the metal desk. Someone took care of them, without saying anything. The janitor, he guessed. In the morning his desk was always clean.

The day before Christmas, his mother had come to visit him at his grandparents' farm. She didn't look so good. Her skin had bumps like a paper wasp's nest and her dark hair was so thin he could see her scalp. When she said hello to him, the breath that found his nostrils told him what she'd been up to. It was the breath that came home with her late sometimes, times when he and Lance had dragged her up the trailer steps and onto her bed, took off her shoes, pulled a blanket up. *She's been hittin' the bottle,* Lance would say, and it sounded so painful, like when Lance hit him in the stomach and sometimes the head, for no reason except he felt crabby.

His mother brought a present but she did not bring his little brother. He hadn't seen Justin for almost a year. Justin would no longer be a baby, and he didn't think he'd know what his little brother looked like if he passed him at the mall or on the street. For all he knew, his mother might not even have Justin anymore, but he was afraid to ask.

The present wasn't big enough or small enough to be something good. It was wrapped in dark green paper with holly berries on it, a shallow rectangle that meant clothes.

When his mother came to the door, his grandparents cleared off to town to do errands. She didn't have a present for them or they one for her. Just a short nod and a hooking of eyes and then they were gone.

She sat across from him at the kitchen table, her gaze pinned to the shiny squares of the tablecloth. "So how you doing?"

He shrugged. Whenever someone asked how he was doing—

his teacher, the principal, the school counselor—it felt like he filled up with air and his brain collapsed.

"We're getting by," his mother said like he'd asked the question. "Aunt Jane and Uncle Bill live in the trailer with us."

Us. She'd kept Justin.

"Wanted to pay something for rent, but I said, 'You kidding?' Should be I'm paying *them,* but I don't have it."

Her gaze went back to the tablecloth. Her fingertips tapped the table but made no sound because the nails were cut short. She had to do that for work, he remembered, because what she sorted couldn't get scratched. "Why don't you open it?" she asked, pushing the present toward him with her knuckle. "Might as well."

He stared at the present, at the holly berries the color of blood. He didn't want to open it now. He wanted to open it later. On Christmas. At the trailer. With her and Justin and Aunt Jane and Uncle Bill.

"You okay?"

Now was his chance. He willed his chest to open, his throat to unstick. Somehow he had to make his voice work. He opened and closed his mouth; three hard shoves the pump handle took to get the water running in the barn. But no matter how hard he heaved, the words wouldn't come.

His mother looked at him. "You don't talk no more, do you?" She nodded. "Easier on your grandparents."

He blinked at her and pushed the present box back her way.

"Spoiled, are you? Don't need nothing?"

He shook his head, not knowing himself if he meant he did need or he didn't.

ELEVEN

SUSAN CAN SEE THE SEARCHERS COMING BACK, A MIXED LOT OF volunteers, a small defeated army. Heads bowed, feet numb and dragging. They are silent now except for the occasional beeps and squawks of their radios that carry so successfully in the cold, clear air. He's dead, Susan thinks. It is one o'clock. She isn't a complete fool. He's had a heart attack. He's gone hypothermic. He's stumbled and broken his head on a rock. He's fallen into a ditch. It feels as though she is being peeled from inside out, sundered, vacuumed, disemboweled.

Over the course of the day so far, their numbers have increased: twenty, thirty, forty. Now it is something near seventy. They keep arriving in station wagons and in trucks. In vans and minibuses. And even though they conduct themselves with dignity once they hit the ground, she has noticed the buoyancy or boisterousness with which they heave themselves out of their vehicles, chests and chins thrust forward like parachuters exploding forward into thin air.

That is, until reality hits like an invisible barricade. This is not a reunion or a rally. This is a mission with a human life at stake. The men cast their eyes down. Hubris blown out one ear or the other. They cluster silently waiting for orders.

Perhaps she should cook something: a huge vat of beef stew, a cauldron of hot chocolate? Perhaps she should call a local church to see about renting a coffee urn. Warm food, comfort food. She turns from the living room window and moves to the kitchen. She gets as far as the cupboard before she feels as though she might collapse. *Be useful.* She can't. It feels all of a sudden like she is going to die.

Jeff appears behind her. From God knows where.

"Susan?"

Her first name. The surprise of that revives her. "I'm trying to think of ways to help. I could make some food. Some soup. Some coffee—" She turns to the freezer where she stores the whole beans.

"That's being taken care of. How about you eat something?" Jeff motions her to sit at the kitchen table and she obeys.

"What are you hearing?"

"Not much."

Two words. Swift kicks to the stomach. She sits down in Christopher's chair, fingering the plastic buckle of the seat belt she fashioned from an old yoga strap. She thought herself so clever that day.

Jeff opens the refrigerator. "What can I fix you? Eggs? How'd you like them? Easy? Omelet? Scrambled?"

"We don't have any eggs," she says. "That's how it started."

"How what started?"

Susan's gaze shifts to a button on the floor which she leans to pick up. It is flat and red with strokes of gold around the rim. "He dropped this," she says. "I gave him buttons to play with while I tried to figure out breakfast. A miracle he didn't eat it. I often wonder what I'm thinking."

"You weren't."

"True."

Jeff places a yogurt container in front of her, beside it, a teaspoon. Next, a mug of tea, a plate of crackers, a jar of peanut butter, and a blunt-edged knife. "Protein, dairy. Good for stress." He seats himself across from her at the table.

Susan smiles. "You'd make someone a good wife."

"Think so?" He rips the foil lid back on the yogurt as though he is popping a beer tab and sets it in front of her. "My wife left me this morning."

"Oh," Susan says, handing back the yogurt. "Then perhaps you're the one who needs this."

"Thanks."

She watches Jeff dip his spoon in the yogurt, his eyelids lowered; it is clear he isn't going to say more. Which is fine with her. If Jeff, the little strong man in his carapace of wool and canvas, were to break down right now, if he were to need *her*, she'd break down as well.

"Great day," Jeff says.

"Heavenly."

Their eyes meet and they want to laugh, Susan thinks. Or cry. But Jeff breaks the gaze. It is neatly snipped. Like feral cats, they sniff up to a point, skitter back. The tip of his spoon dips again into his yogurt, reminding her of the way Christopher used to eat his daily grapefruit in the old days. He turned the pink wheel of fruit, turned and jabbed at it with the tip of his serrated spoon, a Father's Day gift from Peter, jabbing and pecking like an old woman at an embroidery hoop. Perhaps not so delicate.

How can a man attack yogurt as though it were a grapefruit? Each bite seems to cause Jeff as much pain as pleasure.

"What happened this morning?" Jeff asks.

Susan blinks, uncertain whether this is a question for her or for himself. "He had a fit. Over breakfast. He wanted eggs, and we didn't have any. Then I tried to distract him with the Christmas tree, and that didn't work, and then—" She doesn't have to tell the whole story. Those details can't possibly matter. "He had what's called a 'catastrophic reaction.' A serious tantrum. And I needed to recoup my sanity, so I went for a walk. For just a few minutes. When I came back, he was gone."

"Did Christopher ever head for the woods?" Jeff asks.

Did Christopher ever head for the woods? Yes, Christopher once headed for the woods. Not these woods, though.

"He always heads for town. I told you."

"Quite a distance."

"A mile or two. He's a good walker."

Jeff gives her a quizzical look. "You follow him?"

Susan feels heat gather in her cheeks. How to explain this without sounding like a nut? "I'm intrigued by his wanderings. About the whole mechanism.

"You see, the disease affects the hippocampus, the area of the brain that controls a sense of geography, of location, so I became curious as to whether other areas of Christopher's brain might compensate for his loss of function. You know, it might turn out, for example, that he developed a heightened sense of smell. Or sight, or hearing. It might turn out that Christopher developed an animal's instincts or abilities to find his way back home." Home. But where was that? Here? Princeton? Or someplace tucked far in a past he rarely spoke of? An only child (like her) of wealthy parents, sent by them to boarding school—his mind was his home, he used to say. His imagination. And the line went through her head, something picked up from high school English class, "*I dreamt I dwelt in marble halls . . .*"

"Well?"

"No compensation. And the only constant I can determine is that he seems to crave sunlight through plate glass."

"Sunlight through glass?"

"Like a cat. He curls up in it; the warmth soothes him. He loves the old gas station on the corner of Main and Clinton. Seats himself right inside their front window."

"Or he might just like the smell of gasoline."

"True."

Jeff twists, sights the open garbage can and sinks the empty yogurt container.

"Bravo," Susan says, though really she thinks it's a rather childish thing to do.

"Susan," Jeff says, spinning back to face her, his eyes alert. "Is Christopher suicidal?"

"Why do you ask?"

"Suicides behave differently than people who just get lost."

"How so?"

"Sometimes they have plans."

Susan snorts. "If Christopher has plans, they're indecipherable."

Jeff nods. "Still."

Susan swallows a sip of her tea, now grown lukewarm and several shades too dark. "He mentioned it once. Early on. When he was mostly 'there,' so to speak. He wanted to talk about the future, about reasonable steps to take when he started to decline. He was clear as a bell sometimes."

Jeff clears his throat. "What was his plan?"

Susan fixes her gaze on Jeff for an instant. His brow is furrowed, face muscles taut, awaiting her answer. Where did this man come from? Why does he care so much? "I don't know if there was one or if he was improvising."

But it comes back to her in a flash. They were sitting at the dining room table, a month or so after meeting with Christopher's neurologist, when Christopher cleared his throat and set down his wineglass. Lately, they'd been drinking wine in the afternoon instead of tea. They were both a little drunk.

"The best course, I think," Christopher said in the tone he used for clients, warm but deliberate, "is to end it." Then, seeing her look of shock: "I don't mean now. When it gets worse."

He'd misread her expression. For a split second, she'd thought he meant the marriage. Why would she think that? "Worse for who? You or me?" She was furious and hurt and he'd better know it, demented or not.

"For you, of course," Christopher said. "I didn't realize—"

"How am I supposed to do it? Stab you? Poison you? Pop a little pentobarbital in your cocktail?"

"I'm sorry, dear. I wasn't thinking."

"And when I'm hauled in for assisted manslaughter? Premeditated murder? Where will you be to help?" She knew she was sounding loopy, but, she wondered, after all these years did Christopher still think she wanted to get rid of him?

"Sit down," Christopher said. "You're scaring me."

"Ditto," she said. "Ditto. Ditto. Ditto." She stood, arms crossed, looking out the picture window that faced the woods, framing them. Below lay the pond on which they skated in winter, swam in summer. She'd managed to start irises around its fringe when it was first dug. The high green blades rose in early summer like a wattle topped with yellow heads. She had been at this same window, fifteen years before, waiting for the police and their dogs to find Christopher, for the phone to ring in case it might be him. Then, it was late autumn. A gray day. Yellow rafts of beechnut leaves wafted from the tree beside the pond.

"Susan?"

Jeff's voice brought her back to the present. "He did attempt suicide once. A long time ago. I can't see how it's relevant—"

"Attempted?"

"Threatened—"

"What was going on with Christopher?"

Susan blinks. "Do you want the psychological answer or the biochemical one?" She fingers the paper tag dangling from her tea bag. Sometimes there are fortunes in tiny print. Not this brand. "You have no idea what it took for a woman of my generation to be taken seriously in a lab."

"What does that mean?"

"He found out that I was having an affair."

Dick Morton was the new postdoc in her department, thirty-five to her forty-six, she guessed. He had applied to the university to work under her, his research on regeneration in newts dovetailed brilliantly with her own. Love was not expected, was not sought or even desired on Susan's part. What excited her about her affair with Dick Morton was the extraordinary clarity of mind and confidence in her own powers their lovemaking seemed to produce. While some people might fall asleep after sex, Susan flew to her lab, immersing herself in work that before meeting Dick had begun to lag, even to bore—now suddenly was shot with light.

Even her organisms seemed to be responding to her new state of mind. She thought of new experiments, new methodology. She could finally see the possibility of finishing the journal article on intercalation that was so long overdue. In odd moments she fantasized about recognition, a lightning stroke of fame—perhaps even one of those coveted prizes in her field. This, she scolded herself, from a woman who regularly reminded dissatisfied graduate students that the reward was in the work.

On the morning that Christopher discovered a note from Dick on department stationery in her purse (he wasn't snooping, he was rummaging for the checkbook), something lusty, amorous, and totally incriminating, he called the department, got the secretary, a thin weepy woman named Marge, and left a message for Susan: *I know what you've done. I have a knife. I'm going to the woods.*

She was standing at the blackboard, her pointer stabbing the abdominal cavity of a dissected rat, a slide, fifty white-coated students ranged around their own dissected rats on the black-topped tables awaiting her next instruction on how to proceed, when she saw Marge, tearstained as usual, but several shades pinker, fly toward her, shouting for her to come.

The students, flustered, confused, started up in a babble of questions over which Marge shouted, "SHE CAN'T TALK! SHE'S GOT TO COME WITH ME!"

Ten minutes later a police officer met her in her office.

"I've been having an affair," Susan told him. "I assume Christopher's found out." Hard to believe the coolness with which she could say these words. The door to her office was still closed. Marge, for all she knew, could be listening at the keyhole. But who cared? In a community this small, affair gossip was the norm, almost passé. The police presence was not.

"The woods," the officer said. His name was Bart. First or last, she never did determine. "Are there any woods near you? Near your house?"

She nodded. "We're surrounded by woods. My husband's an architect. He selected the site."

It was closing on noon when they reached the house. A warmer day than usual for early November. Good tracking conditions, Officer Bart assured her. They would find him. Her job was to stay by the telephone, he told her. If anyone called, get them off the line. If Christopher called, keep him on. "No matter what he says or what he calls you, be calm. Try to get him to reveal his location. If he hangs up on you, leave the phone off the hook."

"You're leaving me alone?" Suddenly, Susan was terrified.

"Backup's coming. But it's going to be silent. Leave the front and back doors open. We don't want to scare him."

She nodded. She chose to stay by the telephone in the living room because the whole glass side of it faced the woods. She'd stood here so many times, watching Christopher and Peter swimming naked below; watching Christopher clearing the pond in winter. He shoveled for hours in the cold, under the glare of a single floodlight attached to a telephone pole. So methodical, so diligent. He worked like a machine, a rhythmic machine. Peter helped him sometimes, but even Peter eventually grew tired or bored and dropped his shovel on the bank to come inside for hot chocolate and a warm fire.

Christopher had a method. He started at the center and scooped in rays out to the pond's edge. Round and round he went, freeing the smooth surface beneath the crust of snow.

"How can you work so hard?" she had asked him once when he came back in. Christopher's face was deeply flushed and rivulets of sweat coursed down the sides of his temples. Breathing hard, he pulled off the beggar's gloves he'd been wearing, the kind with the tips cut off, revealing his blunt white fingertips. *"Ten frozen parsnips hanging in the weather,"* she thought.

Christopher shrugged and hung the damp gloves on the screen in front of the blazing fire. "I guess I just like to push."

Once the pond was cleared, the three of them skated for hours, each in his own orbit, yet connected, as orbits are.

"Mom?"

Susan started. It was Peter, silent as a cat. "Oh my God, when did you get home?"

"I've been home." Peter stood barefoot at the bottom of the stairs, his lanky torso wound like a vine around the timber post that soared up from the banister. "What are the cops doing here?"

Why was he home? What did that mean? "Dad called my secretary half an hour ago. He says he's going to the woods to kill himself." Should she have told him like that? She couldn't stop herself.

Peter, still grasping the post, shook his head. "Fucked. Up."

She nodded. If he would just come toward her, hold her instead of that post.

"The cops checked his studio?"

She stepped toward him. "Dad's studio? They must have."

"Cops are stupider than you think, Mom. Believe me. Maybe he faked them out or something. Check the studio."

She looked at him. He looked tired. His flannel shirt was askew, buttoned wrong from top to bottom. "Did you see him?"

Peter unwound himself from the post, but did not move toward her. "The studio," he said again, then turned and clumped back up the stairs.

The cut was not deep. A quill scratch across the inside of his right wrist. Only later would she discover the other mark, a tiny bull's-eye above Christopher's breastbone where he'd tested the idea of hoisting himself on his own petard. Both were superficial wounds, requiring no greater treatment than a squirt of antibiotic ointment and a Band-Aid. Yet because there were wounds, the admitting doctor explained to Susan, Christopher would be observed for a week in the psychiatric ward.

It was not until later, much later, after Susan had returned home from the hospital and had heated chicken noodle soup for her and Peter's dinner, that she remembered to ask him why he'd been home.

Peter shrugged. Between slurps of soup he managed to say, "A walk."

"With whom?"

"Myself."

Susan closed her eyes, trying to steady herself. This was not a time to fight. It was the era of runaway children, and Peter, thank God, was not running away, he was *walking*, yet he was supposed to be in school. "You were on a walk. By yourself." Did she believe him? Did it matter? "Have you done this before?"

"Uh-huh."

"Why hasn't anyone ever called me?"

Peter shrugged.

"Why?" She was truly bewildered. "You have a double?"

Peter smiled tightly to himself, keeping his gaze on his soup. The light dawned. "You swiped my letterhead."

Peter brought his head up.

"So where do you go?"

"The woods."

"The woods?"

"I'm learning mushrooms from Jacques."

Jacques. She was the one who'd originally called Jacques, a colleague, a world-renowned mycologist, to ask if Peter could accompany him in the field. She wondered now why she had felt such an urgency to hook them up just as she was becoming involved with Dick. "Oh, you were with Jacques."

Peter began tapping his toe. Christopher's habit, too, when he was nervous.

"Stop that. Please. We need to talk."

Peter lifted his gaze to glare at her. "I don't want to hear your shit, Mom."

The sound of the word, its crudeness, its rushing sibilant of disgust, made her flinch. "Please, Peter, I need kindness."

"Mom," Peter said. His voice dropped. Resonant, resigned. "Mom." He stood up and walked around behind her and began kneading her shoulders.

Her head hung. How could she speak of her gratitude and her need? Peter's arms came up around her as he rested his chin on the crown of her head. His flanneled arms held the smells of moist humus and pine and the unmasked tang of his sweat. Closing her eyes, she mouthed kisses that sounded like little taps of rain. "I'm sorry," she said.

"You should be."

Twelve

After their conversation in the kitchen, Jeff had gone back to the tent to check the "playbook," as he put it. She wondered if this was truly how he viewed the search—as a series of directed moves across a grid, headed for the end zone, the goal. At the end of every game was a sense of completion—or, at the very least, closure. A definite outcome, a win or a loss. And an identifiable opponent. She saw it quite differently. In the way of the ancient Greeks. She saw that there was fate, that there were forces beyond one's control—and at the same time, a mysterious combustion, occurring when hubris interacted with the wills of the gods. Could it be that her hubris in conducting her affairs (not just the sexual one) had offended the gods? That their wrath, vented on poor Christopher, was, in fact, her due?

On their first visit to the psychologist's office for testing, over a year ago, Christopher had been confused and anxious, but eager to make a good impression. He wasn't quite sure, he told the doctor, why he was here. He blamed his wife, he said, who was prone to worry. But it was Christopher's doctor who had ordered the CAT scan, and the consulting neurologist who'd sent them to

Dr. Tealman, Susan reminded him. We need a baseline of your brain functions, he'd said. For future comparison.

Sitting in the waiting room while Christopher took the tests had been agonizing. Even over the white-noise machine humming in the corner, she could hear Christopher cursing his frustration. Later, he told her that when he came to a task he couldn't do and felt like crying, Dr. Tealman had assured him, "You can only do what you can do."

On their second visit to the pleasant office, Christopher seemed calm, almost resigned. But Susan's stomach kinked as soon as she entered the room with its tasteful prints, its row of ceramic teapots, its glossy porcelain head with the brain parts stenciled in black, a bit grotesque, but also intriguing, and a hairline of headache pain cracked her foreskull. They sat side by side in leather chairs, the seats like palms holding them, and she wished that she could just close her eyes and rest there, that when she opened them again, the whole situation would have disappeared.

Dr. Tealman, dressed in khakis and a light blue shirt, swiveled to face them. He was a tall man, the sort of man who was used to folding his length to shorten the distance between himself and his patients, she thought. He greeted them, thanked them for coming (What option was there? Susan thought), congratulated Christopher on his good nature, on taking such a long battery of tests. "I know it can be difficult," he said. "And even humiliating at times—"

Christopher grimaced.

"But you hung in there, did a great job."

Christopher nodded. "Thank you."

"So here are copies of the report. We'll look it over together, and of course I'll try to answer your questions—"

"Does this mean I can't work?"

Susan squinted as pain burst behind her eyeballs, but Dr. Tealman's voice remained steady, like that of a patient father.

"That worries you."

"I'm not ready to be an old man."

Or me, the wife of an old man, Susan thought.

"Well, the good news is that so far the executive functions, your decision-making skills—'the conductor of the orchestra'—are completely intact."

"You mean my brain still works?" Christopher asked.

"Yes, definitely, but I remember you told me that tasks you did very easily in the past, like remembering all the details from the three books you read a week and all the details of your architectural drawings—"

"I'm mainly theoretical now."

Not yet, Susan thought. Not entirely.

"—aren't easy anymore."

Susan put her hand over Christopher's. Not to mention the misplaced keys; the bounced checks.

Christopher cleared his throat. "Can I keep working?"

Susan watched Dr. Tealman's eyelids flutter. He won't give us the truth, she thought.

"I suggest that you have someone handle the details, the paperwork and such, so you don't become overwhelmed."

"You're saying you want Christopher to delegate," Susan said.

Dr. Tealman nodded, and Susan found herself trying to parse the man's near-placid expression. She could not.

Christopher squeezed Susan's hand as he shifted forward in his chair. "How quickly is this going to progress, though? What can we expect? Can it be slowed?"

Dr. Tealman thrust his chin in Christopher's direction and planted his elbows on the desk that stood like a dark hedge between them. "On the positive side, you're in good shape; you get lots of mental stimulation. But it's important to go ahead with the neurologist's recommendation for medication."

Christopher dropped her hand to pinch the ridges of corduroy at his knees. He had told her before they went into the appointment that he wanted to avoid more medication if possible. "It will really help?" he asked.

"Ten to twelve percent improvement. But that means something."

Christopher nodded. "We'll do whatever you recommend," he said.

The moment she entered Johnson Hall, she could have wept with relief. Clean white halls running with enameled industrial piping, a hint of humor in the bright colors juxtaposed with the brisk, clinical lines of the architecture. She pushed the elevator button for "four"—Developmental Biology. Her department, her lab.

Her office was directly opposite the elevator doors. Convenient. No need to make chitchat with Daphne, the department secretary, or any of her colleagues who sometimes left their doors open while they worked, a sort of code to stop in and touch base.

When they got home from the appointment with Dr. Tealman, Christopher decided to go to his studio. He needed to be alone, he said. He needed to digest. She was relieved. She, too, needed time on her own.

She unlocked her door quickly, closing it behind her. She could have had a bigger office, but she loved this one. High-ceilinged, crammed with books. One huge window with a view of the campus gardens beyond, and an aquarium that ran half the length of the far wall in which she kept her rarest salamander, Tillie, an albino axolotl with pink-fringed gills and a dumb, trusting smile. Axolotls had tiny, tiny brains and ten times the amount of DNA of humans, yet when Susan moved to the glass, Tillie swam toward her as though she recognized her. Conditioning, Susan knew; still she tapped the glass and made little clucking noises of greeting. *Dear dumb Tillie.*

Susan's research was on the regenerative properties of salamanders, axolotls in particular, thanks to their enormous capacity for quick regeneration. Indeed, she was credited with discovering that regeneration in salamanders was not based on master control cells, but on individual cells that communicate with one another, signaling and responding, working things out, making biochemical decisions. For years her research had been out of fashion, but with the war and the aging baby boomer population, her understanding of the cellular process in regenerating limbs, hearts, and brains was finally attracting notice and grant money.

From the outside the newtary looked like a walk-in refrigerator with a heavy steel door and a levered handle. Inside, the room was a constant 65 degrees Fahrenheit, a perfect temperature for salamander survival. The shelves were lined with shoe-box-sized plastic tubs, each labeled with the species name, the date of the operation, the student caretaker's initials. At the far end of the small room were three small aquariums, each occupied by an axolotl.

Susan loved this room, a sort of sanctuary. Whenever she entered, she felt herself come awake, her senses sharpened in anticipation of "doing her science." The salamanders were gifts from colleagues all over the world. In one tub was the tiger salamander, *Ambystoma tigrinum*, one of the largest terrestrial salamanders in North America; in another, the delicate blue

Ambystoma laterale; above that, a salamander sent to her from Japan, with three hands that look like tiny trees. In her research, Susan discovered that these deformities that look monstrous to the untutored eye in fact conform to an established pattern that the cells worked hard to preserve.

Today she needed a red-spotted newt, *Notophthalmus viridescens*, found easily enough in nearby woods by the undergraduates in her Intro course. These were the salamanders she'd been using to observe heart and brain regeneration. The operations were surprisingly simple; the results, astounding.

"So you'll see it's disgustingly easy," Susan said as she walked to the table where Jennifer had set up the instruments, a scalpel and a watchmaker's forceps, beside the dissecting microscope.

Jennifer, her blond hair tucked in a bun, nodded. "Well, I appreciate you showing me, Professor Hunsinger. I really do."

"It's great for me. Another trained technician. So let's see your solution."

Jennifer raised a test tube of clear liquid.

"You sure this is 0.1 percent exactly?"

Jennifer nodded. "I put 0.1 grams in one hundred milliliters."

Susan smiled. "That's right. Perfect. Okay. So we take this little critter and we're going to cover him with wet tissues soaked in your solution—" She laid the newt gently on a cushion of wet tissues, then watched Jennifer cover its body. "Good. But don't cover the eyes. Back of the head, forehead, but you're going to leave this little area open where we're going to cut." She pointed to a smooth, speckled patch, directly behind the eyes.

Susan glanced at Jennifer. Her mouth was set, her eyes, focused.

When she had been Jennifer's age, the entire lab had been male, the instructions delivered to her in a clipped and derisive manner by a professor who, it had been clear, doubted she could follow directions. She strived to do the opposite.

"Okay. And we're going to check if the newt is out by pinching his toes like this—" The tiny toes compressed slightly under her touch.

Jennifer smiled. "No wiggle."

"Right. You can also see his heart beating in his throat, and the blood cells moving through his veins."

"Awesome."

Then she set to work, showing Jennifer how to slice a tiny trapdoor at the top of the skull, first scraping back and forth to score the bone, next finding the natural sutures to separate the plates. "Then it flops back like this." Using the forceps, Susan carefully lifted the bone, skin intact, up and back as though it were hinged. "And here's the treasure." Susan peered through the scope as the image of the salamander's brain, a white translucent globe, flooded the computer screen hooked up beside it. "I think of it as a pearl."

"Or a blob of yogurt," Jennifer said.

Susan nodded. "Let's see if you're going to be a neurosurgeon or not. Take the forceps, and you're going to pinch off a tiny amount. Use the right eyeball as a guide."

She rested her hand on Jennifer's wrist, guiding it. "Remember, micromovements."

"What part of the brain is this?"

"Anterior portion of the forebrain and the olfactory lobe."

Jennifer frowned. "I can't keep my hand still."

"It takes practice," Susan said, "a lot of it." She took the forceps. "Watch." Deftly, she pinched and pulled, tugging away a bit of tissue that she wiped on a wad of cheesecloth. *If only she could dig into Christopher's brain like this, pinch out the tangles, pull out the plaques. All in a day's work.*

"You make it look easy."

"That's how you get to Carnegie Hall." Next, she inserted a micropipette into the trapdoor and sucked lightly. "Don't swallow," she said, ignoring Jennifer's grimace. She tossed the pipette in the red bin and straightened. "Almost done. Could you make me a little bandage, please, out of the wet tissue?"

Jennifer tore a piece no bigger than the tip of a cotton swab and patted it onto the salamander's skull.

"By tomorrow, we won't need it. The skin will have sealed over."

"Wow," Jennifer said.

"Yes, but the real wow is what happens next."

"What's that?"

"The cells start to grow back. In a month or so, new brain."

"Why?"

"Why?"

"I mean what is it about a salamander that's so evolutionarily important that it can regrow its brain, when humans—"

Yes, poor humans. "Answer that and you'll win the Nobel Prize."

That night she and Christopher had managed to get most of the way through a dinner of vegetable dumplings and General Tso's chicken when he put his chopsticks down and reached for her hand across the table. "What's going to happen to me?"

Susan drew a breath. So often in life she had spoken when she should not have. So often the habit of truth-telling had been an anchor round her neck, sinking her. In science, the truth always worked. In life, almost never.

She wished that Christopher were a scientist. She wished they could discuss the functions of genetic markers, the possible defects on chromosomes 1 and 14. Horrible as the disease was, they might immerse themselves in the mystery of the defective APP, which somehow altered the processing of the protein that increased the production of beta-amyloid, the indigestible protein that caused plaque. If Christopher were a scientist, fascination, speculation, perhaps even experimentation might have made him feel his life retained purpose. Instead, she must translate from her world to his.

"Will I go crazy?" he asked at last.

I'm the one who's going crazy. You're just demented, she might have quipped. Before. She stroked his hand and forced herself to look at him in the eyes. *To speak or not to speak*. "It's a *memory* problem, honey. A deficit."

"Caused by?"

This is how it was. Sometimes he was completely himself. "Caused by your aging cells."

Then abstraction solidified into something tangible. A letter from the Department of Motor Vehicles, requesting him to appear at the local branch at this time on this date.

"What for?" he asked.

Susan read the letter herself. Baffling. Simply a request to appear.

She drove him to the office. Curious. Worried. Perhaps she should have called ahead. Surprises did not serve them well these days.

The clerk sat behind a cage, a plump woman, middle-aged. She skimmed the letter that Christopher slid to her beneath the grille, then punched his name into her keyboard. All the while, her eyes fixed on the screen.

"You need a road test," she said.

Christopher looked confused. "Did my license expire?"

"You've got Alzheimer's," the woman said. "State law."

"What are you talking about? That's a lie." He turned to Susan. "Tell her," he said. "Tell her they're confused."

Instead of arguing, she took his arm, steered him carefully away from the clerk's window. Dr. Tealman had told them there was no definitive diagnosis, but that was not the point. The house of cards had fallen; how could she prop it back up?

When they got home, they sat on the edge of the bed and then lay down, though it was only noon. He held her; he told her he loved her. He was still capable of this. He was like a drowning swimmer finding the pier. He clung to her in their bed, not sure he was alive, but in those final gasps, certain he had found his salvation.

She, on the other hand, was hearing an echo of her lab student's question. *Why humans? Why us?*

One night not long after Christopher was tested, Susan woke, her heart beating in her chest, in her ears, like some mad driver headed for a cliff; the rest of her, the witless passenger. Inside her head, questions shrieked like Furies: *What if I die first? Who will take care of him? Who will help?*

Beside her, Christopher lay curled on his side, sleeping peacefully, breathing normally. She touched the blanket that covered his shoulders, his torso, his flanks. Her own body was vigilant, her eyes wide open, but in the dark, nothing had changed.

In the morning, she made an appointment with a psychiatrist. Someone her friend Molly Tyne had recommended.

The appointment with Dr. V. was in the early morning. "The commuter's slot," Dr. V. told Susan. She was a commuter of sorts, Susan thought, shuttling from one world to the other.

"What happens when you panic?" asked Dr. V., a woman of late middle age with a deep widow's peak and hair dyed a shiny, shiny black. Her eyes, even behind thick lenses, seemed to Susan terribly keen.

"I see that I'm going down," Susan said. "Christopher and I are going down. No hope. Only we can go down with fear and anger, or we can go down with love. I want to go down with love. But I don't know how."

On the way home, she decided to surprise Christopher with breakfast in bed. "Go down with love," she and Dr. V. had agreed. Appreciate him while you can.

She was standing at the stove when she heard Christopher's feet pounding down the front stairs. He was shouting.

"My clock! My clock's gone! You stole it!"

"Christopher," she said, springing to meet him. "What are you doing?" She wasn't sure what astounded her more, his tone or his nakedness.

"Come," he said, motioning her to follow.

In their bedroom, Christopher pointed to the table on his side of the bed, a polished burl they'd picked up on a trip to Bali years ago. "My clock! Gone!" The surface of the table was empty.

Susan stared at him. "There," she said, pointing to the clock on the shelf above the headboard. "Get dressed."

Back in the kitchen, she found the pancakes scorched and steaming. The stench of burned fat and char permeated the room. "Damn," she said, dashing the pancakes into the sink. The still-smoking skillet she slid onto one of the unused burners. Then she sat down, reaching for the glass of water she'd already poured for herself. The breakfast tray was set; the syrup warmed. She was surprised to find her hand trembling, her heart beating like a tiny urgent hammer beneath her breast. *I should call someone. Who?*

To her surprise, Dr. Tealman took her call immediately.

"He's already on medication," he said. "There's not a whole lot more we can do."

"I understand," Susan replied. "But this was bizarre. Is he going to settle down? Or is this the norm."

Dr. Tealman coughed. "It's all about conditions. Hard to predict an avalanche. But with some experience, you get adept at reading the snow."

In the following months, the tiny speckled corner of Christopher's forgetfulness seemed to flourish and take hold the way the specks of gray-green mold in the master shower had exploded into black-edged splotches that spread across the ceiling like lichen on a damp rock. Recently there had been several complaints from contractors awaiting plans, from customers wanting to see blueprints, from vendors wanting to be paid. Every morning now Christopher grumbled that he was behind in his work, terribly behind, that he felt like a man with his thumb in the dike.

"It's like I can't think anymore," he complained.

"You're tired," she said. "Too much going on."

Christopher frowned. "You're not in my body. In my head. It's like a big wave comes in and washes over everything, washes everything away—names, places. It's so frustrating." He banged his fist against his forehead. "I can't get it back in time. It washes away."

He lost his bicycle twice in one week and was convinced both times that it had been stolen. The first time, she found it yoked to a parking meter in front of their favorite wine store, but Christopher didn't remember leaving it there. The next time, Christopher could not remember his itinerary of the morning even with her prompts. But later in the week, the university police called to say they'd found the bike chained to a rack outside the parking garage.

Every day now it seemed Christopher worried that they weren't invited to this party or that. Parties he'd only learned about by overhearing snips of conversation at the bakery, or at their favorite café. "How do you know for sure?" Susan asked. "Why do you care? You never used to care."

Christopher ignored her. "Our friends don't like us anymore," he said. "It's because of me."

"Why do you say that? You're the life of the party. The host extraordinaire. You're much better at that stuff than I am." This was true. It *had been* true anyway. She would much rather settle in a corner with a drink and one friend or colleague to discuss issues of the day, of the department than make people feel at home.

"They feel sorry for me, Susan. I'm not stupid."

"What makes you think they know?"

Christopher looked at her. "You haven't told them?"

"What do you think? I've been sending out cards?"

He squinted. "Molly?"

She hesitated. She had told Molly. Her closest friend.

He threw up his hands. "Then everyone knows."

"He gave me a look." Susan closed her eyes. "I thought he was going to deck me." She looked down at the single strand of hair she had wrapped around her forefinger. Her own hair, a silvery white cord that caught the light.

"It sounds like the disease," Dr. V. said.

"I was scared."

"Understandable."

"There was a period in our lives when Christopher was incredibly angry at me like that." Oh yes, despite his medication, despite the twice-weekly appointments with his psychiatrist, he would dive into anger, a quick slide from delirium of insight to delirium of rage. *Where've you been?* he'd demand as soon as she got home in the evening, though she might be only half an hour later than her usual. *Tell lover boy I'll kill him if I see him.*

Dr. V. tugged her herringbone skirt toward her crossed knee. "Well, he obviously got over it," she responded.

"How do you know?"

"You're still married."

Yes, Susan reflected. They'd gotten over it. Therapy. Medication Christopher had probably needed for a long time. "Is there such a term as 'collegial sex'? Because that's mainly what it was. A way of making connections, establishing trust. Is that odd?" She turned her head to get a glimpse of Dr. V.'s expression. Weren't they about the same age? Didn't she remember those days? How difficult it was for a gifted woman to make headway?

Dr. V. shifted again, this time scribbling something in the leather-bound notebook she kept on her lap. "Are you still promiscuous?"

Susan blinked. Such an old-fashioned word. A word that her mother might have used, though her mother never spoke to her of matters like these. Her mother was a scientist. As a child, Susan had spent long quiet afternoons in her mother's lab swishing food coloring and water in glass tubes, playing "Madame Curie" while her mother occupied herself with her microscope and her slides. "God, no. This was years ago. Years and years."

"Christopher didn't accept your explanation?"

Susan pulled the strand tighter, watching white bands edge to red along her forefinger. "I made a commitment that I've stuck to—and I'm glad about that."

"So what's bothering you so much?"

Susan nodded. Ah yes, good doctor. Here was the crux. "A thought. A horrible thought. About cells. Cellular fate. I keep wondering if sometime back then, back when—you know—" She closed her eyes, seeing herself standing by the blackboard in the lecture hall, her secretary flying down the aisle, shouting for her to come.

Wasn't it possible that in that crucible of rage, Christopher's cells had rattled off their tracks, lost their bearings, no longer able to determine the good fight?

"You mean you're wondering if your actions caused Christopher's illness?"

On the wall at the foot of the divan hung a small, framed print, rose-colored ellipses outlined in Miró-like black. When Susan closed her eyes, the shapes swam behind her eyelids like parameciums. "Yes," she said. "Cells turn on and off. We don't entirely know why. Stress. Adrenaline. Something in Christopher's biochemistry might have been screwed up when he discovered my affair. It might be my fault."

Saying this aloud made her mind race. Of course it was true, because so many things were her fault, because early one Sunday morning, the Sunday after high school graduation, David Kappelman, on his way home from her house where he had spent the night secreted in her bed, was killed by a driver who ran a red light. It was the first full night he had spent with a woman and she with a man, a night spent nearly suffocating in pleasure and fear. David Kappelman, captain of the tennis team, editor of the school newspaper. Valedictorian. *The Jew who was headed for Harvard.* David Kappelman. Black wavy hair and forearms strong as ironwood.

At dawn, the lovers were up, still intoxicated with the success of their heist, her maidenhood spirited away in a big black sack.

They were up before Susan's mother and father. Susan watched David move through shadow, the whole naked length of him, the muscles of his thighs tensing as he drew up his pants, the conquistador arch of his ribs as he drew on his shirt. The spent condom, wrapped in enough layers of toilet paper to resemble a snowball, he stuffed in his back pocket.

She was not going to lie. She knew the time of the accident almost precisely. He had left her house at 5:30 A.M., she informed the police. The hell with scandal. She wanted the police to have the truth. She was, after all, a scientist in her soul. The facts. Better to live with the facts.

For the rest of the summer, she set herself to reading the Oedipus trilogy, first, in English; then, painstakingly, in ancient Greek. One word had drawn her to the plays, "tragedy." Like Oedipus, fate had cast her beyond the pale, beyond the gates of the city. Her friends, at first, tried to comfort her, but she could not be comforted, not by those whose lives now seemed to her puppet-like, predetermined, strange.

Beside her on the bed, she kept a dictionary and a wooden file box whose interior smelled of cedar. At almost every word, she stopped to look up its definition, then carefully made out a card, the vocabulary word in Greek on one side; its meaning, on the other. At the end of the day, she drilled herself on the tidy cards in the tidy box. Slowly the Greek words stopped swimming; nouns and verbs began to make sense—popping out at her like wild-flowers in the forest undergrowth, beautiful and apparent once your eyes adjusted. All summer she prayed for a place of solace, a refuge sanctified by the gods like Oedipus's sacred grove. But she did not find it.

And here she found herself again in that place of isolation. Antigone leading poor, blind Oedipus along the peripheries of the civilized world. In the year before she'd decided to move,

Susan had been taken aside more than a dozen times. Beckoned into a bathroom, a kitchen, an alcove beneath the stairs. There she met raised eyebrows, furtive shakes of the head. Some of her friends, like those bullying mothers of her past ("You should go out more—David would want you to be happy"), had the nerve to give advice: "Iron deficiency," they whispered. "Crushed coral calcium." "Vitamin E." They offered the names of institutes, experts, therapists. I've won Job's lottery, Susan thought. All the comforters a girl ever needed.

Those same friends rarely called, or if they did, they were trying to lure her away from Christopher. "Join us for tea, a drink, breakfast, yoga." They were attempting to do good, of course. But they couldn't seem to understand that Christopher was still viable—to her, at any rate.

Susan had described to Dr. V. how terrified she was of what was happening to her and Christopher, how socializing in the old way seemed cruel to Christopher. She had vowed not to do it anymore. And yet it was a case of "You're fired, I quit." More and more her invitations were turned down—illnesses ("Wouldn't want to infect Christopher"); forgotten appointments; relatives coming to town. *Please understand.* Of course she understood.

"A choice between love and fear," Dr. V. had responded. "We spoke about that in our first session. Love and fear. It boils down to that."

Lying on the office divan, Susan held up her hands like a dog's begging paws. "Can I get that tattooed?"

Still, it hurt how often her friends had chosen fear. She and Christopher had lived in this town for close to thirty years. They would be missed, everyone said. They. But really it was Susan. Christopher had been missing a good year now—the Christopher they all knew and cherished. The easy part had been telling these well-wishers and old friends that they were leaving. The hard part was refraining from the diatribe she longed to unleash.

A *place of refuge.* Susan presses her fingertips to her temples, elbows on her knees, as she perches on the edge of the sofa. A broken bough of evergreen; a hunter's cabin; a cave of snow. Let the needle dip once more and find its groove; let Christopher remember how to burrow, how to make fire; let Christopher remember how to stay alive.

Thirteen

"What do you see?" Jeff says, coming up behind Susan, who stands before the window overlooking the neighboring meadow and the road's black curve. "Nothing," she says. "No one's come back. I'm worried."

To Jeff's surprise, he feels a sense of shame wash over him, though she states her observation in a flat tone in which he detects no anger. He would like to say, *It's early yet*, but it's not early. Or late. It just is. She told him to "tell it straight" and the straightest he can be right now is silent.

A strange place, Susan's house. No knickknacks. No statuettes, bronzed shoes, photographs. No trophies. Of the animal or human kind. The house smells of nothing familiar to him, nothing even horribly familiar, unless one counts the faint pineyness of dehydrated blue spruce. The Christmas tree, listing slightly, stands in the corner of the living room, its base swathed in a white sheet.

"Shouldn't that come down?" Jeff asks, pointing at the tree. "You don't really want to leave them dried out like that."

"Oh yes," Susan says, turning. "It's a hazard."

"I'd be happy to handle it, if you like."

For the first time since they've met, Susan smiles her gratitude. "Thank you."

At some point, the manual says, you, the searcher, become the beloved one, the one who's safe, trusted. He's the husband now. She's the wife. Not like Leanne, of course. Not like she looked this morning, coming at him, bull-like and strange. He sees her the way she looked that first time. Pale milk skin spattered with freckles the same shade as her hair. Her little nostrils, her enormous brown eyes.

How a person acts under stress is the key to the soul. The state of it anyhow. Its relative newness.

Not that you want to judge. You never want to judge, but you need to read the signs to be prepared. There are yellers, weepers, kickers, ragers. The woman who demanded a psychic be brought in, ignoring the husband who windmilled his arms and banged doors in disgust. Susan will not be loud, he thinks. But she could fall apart.

One thing he's learned: the women always get their way. Mothers, sisters, daughters. In the end, the rescue squad listens to them. Because it's always the women who think they can see the lost boy in his hole of leaves; the lost daughter bound in the trunk of a speeding car; the lost husband poised for flight from a stanchion above dark water. In his experience, the women always see, but they're not always right.

The tree's a bitch. Dried needles cut into his arms and his neck as he reaches through the branches for the trunk whose bark feels scaled and sappy in his grasp. He turns his head to avoid being stuck in the cheek and temple.

"I could get in there," Susan offers. "Loosen the screws."

Before he can say anything, she drops to her belly, scooching herself beneath the boughs like an eager child. "Careful," he says.

No reply, but the scritch of screws unwinding in their sockets.

The tree's weight shifts deeper into his clutch. The bark scales bite into his naked palm. "Better move," he says. Susan wriggles out from under the tree, brushing spruce needles from the front of her sweater as she stands. "You can swing it around and drag it out the front door."

This is just what he's doing, pivoting the dead tree on its axis like a compass needle, then lowering it to transfer his grasp to the bare trunk.

"Watch the coffee table!"

He stops in time to avoid backing into the table, which she scrambles to push out of his path.

"Oh," she says. "This is more than I bargained for."

He nods; *more than you bargained for.* It's not clear to him if her repentance is sincere or not. Susan opens the front door as he steps back through it dragging the tree by its bare trunk. The boughs fold up neatly as the tree slides through the open frame, over the sill, down the front steps to the walk that bisects the frozen yard.

"Where'd you want—" Before he can finish his sentence, his heel hits a glazed patch on the slate walk, the tree trunk springs loose from his grasp, and as he falls backward, Jeff remembers suddenly a fall from a bolting horse when he was a boy, his instant decision to *let himself fly.*

When he wakes, Susan is crouched beside him, looking concerned but not panicked, he notes, not even slightly panicked.

"Should I call someone over from the tent?"

"Was I out?"

Susan shakes her head. "Five, ten seconds. No more."

"Good."

Then, to his surprise, she is reaching toward him, and he feels her bare palm smoothing the top and back of his head. Caressing him. It feels good.

"No blood," she says. "Can I give you a hand?"

"No." He's already tested his fingers and toes. Now he rolls slowly onto his side, ignoring the fresh pain in his lower back as he pushes himself to his hands and knees. Long ago, when Leanne was pregnant, she showed him how to get up like this without straining anything. She'd learned how to do it in Lamaze class. He'd liked that. Even after they lost the baby, he'd seen her doing it. Getting out of bed like that, getting out of the bathtub after it drained. As if her belly's cargo and the need to protect it were still present.

"You're really not well, are you?"

Jeff, on all fours, looks up at her. It's then that he smells the fecal cloud he's released, pungent as a blast of new silage.

"You can step in the shower," she says. "I've got his clothes. They'll fit, you know. It's an odd thing, but you're about his size. Get up now. Don't worry. Doesn't bother me. I'm trained as a scientist, but after what I've been through, I could be a nurse."

That is how Jeff finds himself soaping with a soft washcloth in a hot shower, then drying himself with a towel so soft and dense that the water on his skin seems to disappear. To his embarrassment, Susan has hung fresh clothes on the back of the door, Christopher's clothes. A pair of dark corduroy trousers, a light wool shirt gridded with orange lines. She put out a pair of socks, too, though certainly he could have worn his own. And underwear. A T-shirt with a V-neck. Black boxers.

He shakes his head, and a spasm of anxiety twists in his gut. How's Christopher? And even as his own skin tingles with well-being, he prays that Christopher's internal thermostat is functioning, that the extreme cold hasn't become extreme heat as the blood vessels expand and the pores gape open. And Corey. Oh

Christ, he forgot that he has to make that call. Jeff runs a finger down the furrows of a corduroy leg, touches a shirtsleeve. He's never worn clothes like these. Professor clothes. He feels like an imposter or a fugitive as he draws the pants, soft as pajamas, over his legs; buttons the shirt. In these clothes, no one would ever recognize him; he doesn't even recognize himself.

He stuffs his soiled pants, his underwear, in the dark plastic bag she left on the towel rack. *A nurse,* she said. She's seen it all. So has he. Or thought he had. His head hurts despite the Advil he swallowed, twice the normal dose. A dull one, relentless, like someone's hammering a wedge of wood behind his eyeballs. Won't stop. He runs his hands over his chest, down his thighs, amazed all over again at his new sleekness, his new pelt. The Indians talk of shape-shifting and this must be it. Before he was a badger, or a bear, now he's a mink. Only the pain in his head reminds him of who he really is.

Combing his hair with his fingers, he notices that he could shave. But that's ridiculous. He can't use Christopher's razor. Or can he? He cracks open the medicine chest. Yes, there it is. Blue, disposable. She must have an entire pack somewhere, out of sight, out of danger. He can't resist. He hasn't felt this clean and comfortable in years, maybe ever.

There's not much to shave, but enough that when he's finished his cheeks feel as smooth as the rest of him.

When he emerges from the upstairs bathroom, she is standing outside the door as though she'd been listening.

"Any calls?"

"No, but in the time you were showering, more troops have mustered. God, I wish I could do something."

"Don't worry," Jeff says. "It's under control, but I've got to get out there."

She looks like she wants to say something, to add something.

Can I go, too? But even for Susan, the stoic, the question has only the force to part her lips.

"Won't be long," Jeff says. "And I'll come back with news." *Hang in there, Christopher.*

"I prefer no news," Susan says. "Unless it's good."

Jeff looks at her for a moment, then nods.

FOURTEEN

THE NIGHT JEFF MET LEANNE, THE MEN AT THE BAR HAD BEEN buying her drinks. Shots of tequila, she favored. Worm piss, they called it. They loved watching her toss them down, trying to pretend the world didn't spin. Clearly they thought she was a good time, a good sport. Might give as good as she got. Girls were always coming and going at Earl's. Farm girls they'd known all their life, and trailer trash like Leanne, stray girls come out of nowhere, who'd rub against you like they wanted you to take them home.

He'd never noticed Leanne before that night, but once he did, he couldn't take his eyes away. She was wearing tight jeans, a black tank top. The men were packed around her so tight he didn't know how she could breathe. Yet she was laughing at whatever the men were saying to her, laughing and pushing back her hair with the hand that didn't hold her drink. She was pretty with a wide face and a freckled, turned-up nose. Large, dark chocolate eyes.

And her hair—oh my God, Jeff thought when he saw it—there were breeds of horses that could grow manes like that, new-penny red, copper-bottom red, a tumbling abundance, like a bushel of apples overturned. You had to be looking at her straight on to glimpse the face taking refuge in there.

And that's what he found himself desiring to do, so fiercely desiring. Aware as he was that he was drunk, too. The right kind of drunk, where you feel your best self rising inside you like a warm, doughy bread. He watched her get up from the bar stool to go to the bathroom. On the first step, she swayed as though her bones had melted, then she managed to catch herself and walk on.

The men paid no attention to her leaving them. While she was with them, she was a package they wanted to open. But once she left, they were distracted by fresher scents: the music and talk and drink and the other women who seemed to buzz more loudly once the queen was gone.

From where Jeff stood, chest tight against the bar, he was content to wait and watch. He was as greedy as the others, he knew, but what he'd been through in 'Nam had taught him when to stand back. He knew there was a way men heated up in situations like this. First, the one burned, then the next and the next; sheer proximity made combustion inevitable. It could happen here. Could happen anywhere. Given the right tinder.

Parting the crowd on her way back from the bathroom, Leanne was noticed again. Maybe the other women weren't as enticing, maybe a hint of boredom had set in or the men were just drunker. "Where you been, honey? What took your ass so long?" Suddenly there were hands pulling her in. "Going for a ride," someone shouted, and several men stood, lifting Leanne over their heads and setting her on top of the bar like a statuette.

Standing up there, Leanne looked pudgier, less majestic than the blazing goddess any of them might have imagined. The top of her jeans had been left open or come unsnapped and a pinch of white panty was caught in the zipper, threatening to wedge it loose. But her expression was game, and when she tilted to one side, then steadied herself, she hooted like a girl stunned by her own athletic feat.

Her enthusiasm buoyed the men, who hooted back, whistling and calling for Leanne over the blare of the blues to *shake it, peel it, let it all hang out.* In an instant, Coy Tyler hoisted himself onto the bar and began to dance a slow one with Leanne. Jeff and all the other men watched Coy grip her denimed ass beneath the shaggy tips of her hair, snugging her crotch to his as he moaned and gyrated to make a show.

"Quit hogging, Coy," someone shouted.

"Best leave us some."

A few of the women spun off their stools and tottered to the bathroom. But if their actions were designed to trigger protest, they didn't work. Instead the crowd pressed farther forward, filling the gaps. Jeff slipped onto one of the newly emptied stools. *Leave us some. All us starving boys.* Coy's hands were massaging up Leanne's back, under her shirt, under her hair. He was working on something, something on the onlookers' behalf, while Leanne pretended not to notice or didn't notice. *But she must know what's happening,* a voice in Jeff's head protested. *She must feel the roughness of Coy's fingertips on her skin, the heaviness of her hair on her bare back as his hands push up shirt and hair, skin over rib.* Slowly, tenderly almost, his fingers worked until they reached her shoulder blades and fanned along the bone.

Then, like he'd touched a button, Leanne stretched her arms above her head like a little girl asking to be undressed. Deftly, Coy slipped the tank top over her head, while the men watched her face disappear, then her hair, the long ends drawn up through the black hood of fabric.

Jeff swallowed and someone loosed a low whistle and others gushed curses of admiration and disbelief. It seemed like a long time, but in fact it was only a short time that Leanne's breasts came into full view, white as skinned pears in the dim light of the bar.

A second later Leanne woke from her spell, grabbing her shirt from Coy and clutching it against her chest as she tried to climb off the bar.

"Where you going, young lady?" "What's the rush?" "We *like* what you showed us." Someone reached out and caught an ankle, bringing Leanne down hard on her backside on the bar, and the men were after her like a loose heifer, fair game, scrambling up onto the bar to pin her shoulders, her legs.

That's when it came to him. *Diversion.* Something he learned in 'Nam. Jeff grabbed his mug and heaved it across the bar above the row of bottles lined like sentinels beneath the mirror. The mirror exploded, glass splinters flying through the air like tiny darts, striking here, there. The men on the bar rose up like angry bulls, swatting, glaring, dazed by the sight of their own blood.

But there was time, just enough time, for Leanne to drop behind the bar and escape out the kitchen door, just enough time for someone to call the police and someone else to call an ambulance. And just enough time for Jeff to leave the scene, knuckle-punching each tabletop he passed on his way out of the bar. Outside in the cool night air, his veins still fizzed and hissed. He wanted to scream and dance at the same time. He wanted to fuck someone, but there was no one to fuck.

The next time he saw Leanne was at the Quickway. She was behind the checkout counter; he was in front, a customer.

He'd been surprised to see her there. He'd thought her young enough to be in school—later he'd learn she'd just dropped out—and he'd imagined somehow that when she ran that night, she'd run forever.

Beneath the fluorescent lights, she looked paler than he remembered. Paler and waxier—almost a dead woman. He could see a fringe of white hairs on her upper lip coated ever so lightly with a shade of flesh-colored powder. She wore her hair back, a huge ponytail that reminded him of a wind-tangled mane. When she glanced up at him to announce his total purchase, he saw that her brown eyes held tiny specks of darker coffee.

He handed her a ten-dollar bill. "I know you."

"Yeah?"

"Earl's. Couple weeks ago."

Her face tightened as her fingers dipped into the penny tray to fish up his change. "You one of the assholes tried to grab my tits?"

He couldn't exactly tell her what really happened, couldn't exactly enlighten her as to his own heroic deeds. The way he was raised, you didn't brag. But the color he turned must have said a lot. At her break she joined him at one of the molded-plastic tables in the back and didn't eat anything, though he offered to pay.

"I heard some guy, some crazy, threw a punch, caused a riot," she said. "Was that you?"

He nodded. She did not mention his bravery, his diversionary tactics.

"Thanks."

He could not speak. Instead, he watched her smoke and drink her Diet Vanilla Coke. Slowly, not so much that day, but the next and the next, she started telling him things.

She'd left home not so long ago, the night of the party at Earl's (that's how she chose to remember it—as a party), after she caught it from her pa, drunk, of course. Caught it real bad. Usually she could get away, but maybe she was too tired from running already that night. He had his belt out and what he wanted she refused to give.

Since then she'd been living in barns, friends' trailers for a night or two. She stole garbage; ate the leftover pizza from the tiered pans on the Quickway counter, the leftover pretzels hard as rocks. Sometimes on purpose she'd rip a hole in a bag of corn chips or cheese popcorn as she was stocking the shelves and pretend to find it. What couldn't be sold was stashed behind the counter for munching on when business was slow.

What else did she eat? Leftover hot dogs broiled to rubber. Leftover half-moon cookies stale as the box they were delivered in. From time to time, Tim, the manager, would tell her to choose a drink. Leanne chose Diet Vanilla Coke.

Her paycheck went to cigarettes, gas money for whomever gave her a ride, and the occasional slice of pizza. Barns were surprisingly warm, she told him. When the animals are in and you've covered yourself with hay.

She could have stayed with her sister if her sister's prick of a husband didn't come on to her every time she got near him.

It wasn't the first time she'd left home, either. She'd been in a foster home once. And she hadn't minded. But she was kicked out. Not because of what she did, but because of what she didn't. The boy she refused to fuck managed to convince the foster mother she was no good.

For a long time she hadn't trusted anybody, she said.

Could that change? Jeff longed to ask. Watching her smoke across the table, he didn't think so. He'd never seen anyone her age smoke as hard as that, as if the smoke were nourishing her lungs, not harming them.

After a week of talking to her, he knew he liked her. He couldn't help himself. She was beautiful; she was smart. She was a survivor. Like him. After Vietnam, and even before, he knew what it was to be alone in the world, though to be fair, Leanne had never said she did feel alone. He had an apartment and a decent enough income. So he asked her if she would like to stay with him. For a while anyways. He'd do as much for a stray cat. And a human being was so much more than a cat.

She said yes. Actually, she'd dragged out the words, "All right," in a tone you couldn't call gracious. But Jeff was happy, happier than he'd thought he could be.

He knew Leanne didn't particularly like him. That even though women told him he was good-looking, he was an old man to her. Staying at his place was just a step higher than sleeping in barns and cadging from the garbage bins outside the school cafeteria. He saw where her gaze went when she walked into his apartment the first time: refrigerator, stove, coffeemaker. She said, "Better not try nothin'."

He didn't. Not for a long while. Not until one night after he'd fixed them both supper—nothing fancy: soup from a can; elbow noodles with butter and salt—when she'd told him that he was growing on her.

She always said he'd rescued her. He was her shining knight. No. She'd never said that. He'd wished she had. A fantasy he could not rid himself of no matter how hard he tried. He *had* rescued her: they both knew it. From what her daddy did. Backwoods people. They should have known better but didn't.

She never said anything direct about that, either. He'd read it, in her eyes, sometimes, if he touched her the wrong way. In the way she seemed to live what had happened in her dreams, calling out, shivering, the sweat of terror pricking her arms. He knew those kinds of dreams.

Like Leanne, he never knew what might make him remember. Sometimes a smell. Or a snippet of song. Sometimes just the sight of something ordinary, only looked at slantwise. Last week, he'd reached for a cellophaned package of chicken parts at the supermarket, and all of a sudden he was seeing arms, legs, torsos, heads, mixed parts they'd had to bag after the Chinook he'd cleared for takeoff exploded over the trees. Thirty-seven dead. Hundreds of parts to sort and bag and send home as a single human package.

In the privacy of his parked car, Jeff had brought his forehead to the rim of the steering wheel and keened like those village elders, men and women, he'd seen so many times bent over the bodies of their dead.

FIFTEEN

INSIDE THE TENT, THE HEATER IS BLASTING, THE MEN STAND-
ing, stomping, holding mugs of coffee, Styrofoam bowls of soup.
The usual wives are here helping out, not so difficult on a Friday
morning after New Year's, a good pick-me-up in the middle of all
the letdown.

Leanne used to help out in the beginning, but she didn't like
it much and the others, the other women, that is, didn't much
like her. Too young, he suspected. Too pretty, the way her hair
flared out over the black leather jacket he'd bought her for the
wedding.

Maybe it was her looks. Maybe it was her attitude. She just
couldn't stop talking about how she'd rather be out tracking with
the boys, doing the fun stuff, than playing June Cleaver in the
warm-up tent. A few probably agreed with her, but no one really
stirred. Leanne always said she liked men better than women.
She said it a lot and she said it out loud. He never could understand why she felt that way given what she'd been through. He felt
just the opposite.

A folding table is pushed up to one side of the tent and Higgs
and some other officers are standing over it. On the surface,

they've unfolded a topo map whose edges drape over the corners of the table like a cloth.

"Hey," Jeff says, shouldering his way in. "What're we seeing?"

Higgs pauses an instant to give him a nod. He is drawing a bright pink line across the map, connecting ballpoint X's. "All that's clear road," he says.

"Clear? What do you mean? No tracks? Clues?"

Higgs taps his ballpoint on the map. "We searched it and there's nothing. So we're going to have to start a grid across the bottom part here—" He touches the map again with his pen; this time the cap is on.

"Only there's a ravine through there, real steep, and you need a special team, which you don't have."

Higgs straightens, sticking his pen in his breast pocket. "What do you recommend, Herdman?"

"Bring in the helicopter while there's still a chance to pick up movement, body heat. Can I see the briefing record?"

Higgs tilts his head in the direction of the food table. "Wiltsie borrowed it."

Jeff raises his eyebrows. "Wiltsie's here?"

"Everybody and his neighbor's here, Herdman. How's it going inside?"

"Pretty steady. She's alone in there. Except me."

Someone waves from the rear of the tent. Wiltsie.

"You'd best be going back then, Herdman. You're the only guy we can spare."

Jeff gazes down at the mottled floor. All the men's boots have packed the snow hard and gray. "If the temperature drops any more, you have to take the guys out, so what about a copter?"

"Okay, it's coming."

Jeff scuffs some more. "What about parking some vehicles across the fire roads and the power lines? Anyone mention it?"

"Do you know how much that costs the county? Locking down all those men and cars?"

Jeff shakes his head. "It'd be great if the county put the bucks into rescuing someone."

"I'll pretend I didn't hear that; you pretend you didn't say it."

"Let me see the map again."

"Sorry. You've got your orders, I've got mine."

At the back of the tent, Tina Rawlings is overseeing the coffee urn, two Crock-Pots, and a platter stacked with doughnuts. She is a small woman in a dark blue jumpsuit outlined in fluorescent piping, EMT gear, and snowmobile boots. Her sandy blond bangs nearly cover her eyes. Jeff has always liked her. She makes her living cleaning houses, but she would like to work roads. She keeps putting in her application; the supervisor keeps turning her down.

Now she hands him a cup of coffee, blinking at him through her bangs and asking how it's going.

"It's going," he says. He should hand the coffee back, leave the doughnut where it is. But he doesn't want to call attention to himself, to his miserable stomach, the stomach that's keeping him from where he should be—out in the field, leading the search.

Tina seems to read his mind.

"The Red Cross donated bottled water," she says. "Want that instead?"

He nods, relinquishing the cup of coffee, but still holding the doughnut.

"I've got crackers for the soup." She hands him the wicker basket filled with cellophane packages. "They're the good ones," she says. "Little pillows the kids like."

Gratefully, he stuffs a handful in his pocket. "Keep warm, Tina."

"Good chance of that," she says, rubbing her gloved hands and stamping her feet like a pony. "I feel sorry for those guys in full gear. What 'n hell were they thinking?"

"They weren't thinking; they were posing." Why isn't she in charge of the fire department? Too smart, of course. Too god-damn smart.

At the end of a bench, Wiltsie is poring over the briefing record.

"Anything?" Jeff asks.

Wiltsie shakes his head. "Nada nada and nada. You're the one should be out there. You and Luke and Dan. What I get here is any track he could've left's been trampled by fifty men and a team of elephants. Where's your hasty?"

"Jersey. Weddings."

"People still do that shit?"

Jeff unscrews the cap of the water bottle and takes a slug. "Did you stop at the office?"

Wiltsie shakes his head. "Why?"

Jeff sighs, recaps the bottle. "Corey Byer's being chucked."

"Byer? Kid who burned out his family?"

"He's been living with the grandparents, but I guess they got a problem. Grandpa called this morning. Haven't had time to call him back." But he's got to find time somehow. This means trouble. A shitload. "I'm the liaison with the spouse. She's alone in there."

"No family? Friends?"

"Long story." He gazes at the doughnut he's still holding, watching as his thumbnail pierces the toffee-colored skin through to the pale insides. "Wiltsie," he says. His voice sticks in his throat, too raspy to be understood. "Wiltsie—" A piece of doughnut breaks off and falls to the ground. "I've got to talk to you."

"What?"

"She's gone. She's left me—"

"Jesus!" Wiltsie says, cutting a look of horror at him. "Jesus, cover your face. And get out before Higgs sees you."

Behind him, he hears Tina asking and Wiltsie shushing and then he is out of the tent and back into the frozen air, the slap he needs to get himself together to return to the house.

"Hey, there! Got a minute?"

Coming toward him, the woman reporter from the *Daily Trumpet*. She's wearing an olive-drab parka with a huge fringe of fur, and dark sunglasses pushed back in her hair, so that he has the impression that after this gig she plans to climb on a dogsled and yell "Mush."

"Roberta," she says, thrusting a gloved hand at him and tilting forward. "Roberta Lyons, *Daily Trumpet*. We've probably met."

"Jeff Herdman. We have." He hopes his streaming eyes reveal nothing but the severity of the weather.

Roberta stares at him a moment, then nods. "Oh yeah, the kid. The fire. Right." She clears her throat, clears away that particular memory, which even for her, Jeff imagines, is hard to take. "So I thought maybe we could talk before I go inside—"

"Sure." The truth is that he needs a break, needs to be part of his old milieu.

"You guys been at it since noon?"

"Thereabouts. If you want the exact time, it'd be in the briefing log."

"Which is—"

"Higgs's got a copy in the tent."

"Lieutenant Higgs. My favorite alpha."

Now it's Jeff's turn to clear his throat, covering his smile with his gloved fist. "Yes, ma'am."

Roberta nods and her long, graying hair, despite the sunglasses, flops across her face as she scribbles in a spiral-bound notebook. "Who besides police, fire—"

"Volunteers. Edmonton, Meredith, Colliersville. You probably heard it's an all-county. Helicopter's coming from DEC."

"Damn cold," Roberta says. "How long can a person survive? An older person."

"Depends. Circumstances. Individual's condition. What he's wearing, if he's found shelter." He feels pinpricks beneath his arms, churning in his stomach. Has he said too much? Probably. He always says too much, he realizes. That urge to be important. Searchers all know what not to say. You don't talk about the cold, you don't talk about the response time, or the speculations of what might have happened and who might be to blame. You are all doing the best you can and you are always optimistic but you don't predict anything. Let the future bring what the future will bring.

Roberta tucks her hair behind both ears, sights him with her chin. "So you're telling me it's been four, five hours?"

Watching her, Jeff thinks of Leanne, whose ears stick out like that when she pushes her thick hair behind them. Beyond that, there is no resemblance. "Going on five," he says. "Guys are getting frostbit out there."

"I know this is confidential," Roberta says, locking his gaze. Her eyes are shiny like a cat's. "But how'd the old man get away? Why's it taking so long to find him? What're his chances?" She pushes her face closer to his, drawing her shoulders forward as though she's chilled. "Tell me the truth," she says. "Rescue or recovery?"

Jeff holds his breath. Tragedy makes good copy, he knows, and he is just off center of that tragedy. "The truth is we don't know yet."

Roberta is just opening her mouth to ask another question when Jeff spots Tina coming out of the tent, waving to catch his attention.

"The library called," she says. "I thought you'd want to know. Someone had the bright idea of examining the surveillance tape. Christopher's not on it."

"Thanks, Tina."

Roberta holds her pencil poised as though to spear something. "News?"

"Not really. Now listen, I'll go ahead, make sure Dr. Hunsinger's up for this."

"I'll be here."

Sixteen

As soon as Jeff leaves for the briefing tent, Susan picks up the phone, dials a pattern she knows like a jingle.

"Department of Developmental Biology. May I help you?"

"Daphne."

Susan hears her former secretary's shriek on the other line. "Susan! Where the hell have you been? Are you in town?"

"No. No. I'm—" Where is she? "Here. Up where I live."

"Oh." Daphne sounds truly disappointed. "'Cause I thought, what a coincidence, you calling and this being my last day. We're having a party. Of course, you'd be the star . . ."

"Your last day?"

"I got my master's, at last. Got a real job—not that this wasn't *real*. Too real, sometimes, if you know what I mean. So how're things with you? Oh wait, another line's ringing."

In the silence, Susan presses her fingertips against her cheek. Her cheek feels so soft, her fingertips suddenly freezing. She could hang up now, it would probably be wise. Truck engines rev to life outside; one of the men is announcing something on the bullhorn.

"Sorry, I'm back. Student, of course. Ass on backwards. How do some of them get into this school?"

Susan attempts a laugh, but no sound comes out.

"You still there?"

"Yes."

"So how are things? You making out? We miss you. I miss you. I don't think Doug Hammer misses you—I can't believe what he's done to your office—the students definitely miss you. About three times a week, some kid comes in to ask if they can take your seminar—Susan, you there?"

"Yes."

"It's going okay?"

Susan feels her chest tighten. She'd better get off the telephone. "*Ça marche.*"

"Huh?"

"It goes."

Susan can hear Daphne's hum as she digests this.

"You sound kind of down."

"Well, considering—"

"Yeah, considering. So Christopher's—?"

Susan blinks, the band around her chest tightens and tightens.

"Well, listen, I don't want to make it worse, but I'm probably the only one who'll tell you. Tillie—"

" 'Tillie—'?"

"She died yesterday. Freaky you called. Some dumb-ass kid spilled solution into her aquarium and waited until the end of class to mention it. She got moved into the lab, you know. Doug didn't want her, said she reminded him of his ex-wife, so you can see how lucky *she* was to get rid of him.

"Well, she lived a good life. Tillie, I mean. The student's a wreck. He and some other kids are trying to come up with some sort of scholarship-memorial deal. I'm sure you'll be getting an e-mail—Susan?"

To Susan's horror, she can hear her own bleating sob burst loudly into the phone.

"Susan? Oh God, I'm sorry. I forgot how attached—I—"

On the other end of the line, Susan is shaking her head, mouthing the words, *It's not that, it's that my whole fucking world is coming to an end.*

"Oh shit," Daphne says. "Now I've got to put you on hold, but hang in there—"

As soon as the line goes quiet, Susan hangs up and begins to weep.

SEVENTEEN

"You've been sleeping," Jeff says, touching her shoulder.

"No. What? Have I?" Susan props herself up on her elbows, eager to shake off the impression that she's only half alert.

"It's okay. You need the sleep, but someone's here to see you."

"Who?"

"Roberta, from the *Trumpet*. I figured you called her."

Susan blinks. "I didn't."

"Well, she's here. Do you want to talk to her? I can take care of it if you don't."

"She's here now? In the house?" Susan pushes the hair back from her face, blinks again, but she still feels as though she's looking up at the world from the bottom of a murky pond.

"She's in the command tent talking to Higgs, I guess. I told her she couldn't come in until I'd cleared it with you."

"Thanks. My bones ache and my head's filled with sand, but I guess I better talk to her."

"Want me to stick around?"

"Sure. Any tips?"

"Don't tell her anything—especially what she wants to hear—"

"Which is what?"

"Put it this way—as long as there's hope, there's a search."

The reporter looks like a mountain woman to Susan, someone she imagines spends long stretches of time chopping wood and stacking it. Someone who could as easily join the tracking team as report on it. The scent of cigarette smoke clings to her flannel shirt and around her neck dangles a camera, and something that Susan thinks might be a bottle opener.

Roberta catches her glance and lifts the gadget for her inspection. "For paint lids. Prying them open. I was working on my daughter's room when my editor called me in." She turns to face Jeff, who has come up with a chair for her. "I guess this one's getting some serious attention."

Jeff nods. "Fire, police, DEC."

"K-9?"

"Maybe."

"Damn cold out there." She turns her attention back to Susan. "Sorry, you must be flipping out."

Susan straightens her spine. "I try to keep myself under control."

"Dr. Hunsinger's been great," Jeff says.

" 'Doctor'? So you're really on top of what's going on."

"No, I wouldn't say so. I think Jeff and the others are the ones on top of things. I guess I'm just hoping Christopher finds his way back home."

"You've lived here how long?"

"Going on six months." Susan watches Roberta's heavy eyebrows arch as she scribbles this down.

"Why'd you come?"

"It was far away."

The eyebrows go up again. "From where?"

Susan sighs. "From where we lived."

"Just trying to get the story out, get out the word, so details are nice."

"Details, of course. I'm sorry," Susan says. "Christopher and I moved here from Princeton, New Jersey, where we were both professors. I'm a biologist; my husband's an architect. When he got sick, I felt we needed a change."

"I hear he's done this before."

"Yes, he's wandered before and I've found him."

"You can read the report on all that, Roberta," Jeff says, touching her arm.

"I have. So what happened this morning?"

"We were getting ready to go out for breakfast, and I left my husband for a minute. When I got back, he was gone."

"Wow," Roberta breathes. "Happens quick."

"Five minutes. Maybe ten."

"I get it."

Get what? Susan wonders.

"Doors were unlocked?"

"I don't lock them. He gets too agitated." The last time she locked the doors, he paced back and forth from door to door, trying to twist the knobs first in one fist then the other, screaming at her to "Open, open!" And when she wouldn't obey, he knelt in front of the door and opened his mouth and tried to swallow the doorknob whole.

"So Mr. Hunsinger's been missing, what? Four, five hours?"

"Going on five," Jeff says.

Susan closes her eyes. Five hours. It feels like a lifetime.

Suddenly Roberta jerks up from whatever she's been scribbling on her pad and leans in so close that Susan can see jellyfish-pale lenses floating on the domes of her corneas, the glistening pink rims of her lower lids.

"Do you think he's still alive?"

Often when Susan has listened to celebrities being interviewed about their personal lives on radio or television, she finds herself wondering why these people are so diligent about offering up their autobiographical truth, their family secrets. Why not lie? Why not reinvent the facts instead of giving the interviewer the rope with which to hang you?

"Of course he's alive. That's certain."

Roberta straightens. "Why is that certain?" Her eyes gleam with interest.

"They haven't found him dead."

"Good luck." Roberta offers her large hand first to Susan and then to him. The interview took no longer than fifteen minutes, but Jeff can tell that Susan is exhausted.

They sit in silence, feeling the slight tremor of the front door closing hard behind Roberta. Susan lifts her gaze to him, stretches her fingertips to touch his thigh. "You're good."

"I'm good?"

"Don't you know that? You're uncommonly patient. And not dumb, either."

Jeff cannot help but smile. "Does that mean I'm smart?"

"Now you're taking liberties."

"You're right."

"I guess what I'm trying ever so feebly to say is thank you. For standing by. I wouldn't have thought I'd have needed it, but I do. We're a team—"

"Well, glad I could be here—" He's about to add, *It's my job*, but stops the words before they leave his mouth, knowing they might hurt her. "When do you think you might call your son?"

"Peter? I've tried. An answering machine in the middle of

nowhere. It can't be, can it? 'This is Peter Hunsinger. I can't get to the phone right now. I'm either checking out elephant dung or recording the mating call of a randy rhinoceros. But if you leave a name and message, I'll get back as soon as I can.' He's nuts, he really is."

Or is she? Jeff wonders. People lose it under stress like this. "But the others? You must have friends back where you're really from."

"'Really from.' There's an interesting phrase. Does anyone know where they're really from? I used to feel most comfortable on the pig farm my parents sent me to in the summers when I was a little girl and then at my great-uncle's boatyard in Maine."

"Any relatives?"

"Only children of only children. One of our bonds."

"Friends?"

"Most of our friends are older. Christopher's age. What are they supposed to do? How could they help? It would only worry them." She sighs. Of course her old friend Molly would come if she called her. But she can't bring herself to pick up the telephone. She keeps seeing the expression of unmasked irritation on Molly's face. Toward the end of the going-away party Molly had thrown for them, Christopher had acted bizarrely. Startled to anger over being interrupted by an offer of crabmeat hors d'oeuvres, he'd knocked the student waiter's tray out of her hands and the girl had burst into tears. The apologies and good-byes that ensued had been as hasty as though she and Christopher were running late for a train. "I wish Peter were here, though." She closes her eyes, resting her temples on her fists. "Oh, Peter."

She lifts her face to look at him. "Where are you from?" And when he doesn't answer: "You haven't said much about yourself."

"Curious?"

"I am, and well aware that I'm overstepping my bounds. But it's your job to keep me distracted, isn't it? Distracted, hopeful?"

"You don't want to hear my story then."

Susan raises her eyebrows, expectantly. "I know about your stomach problems. And your wife. Is there worse?"

When he laughs, Susan continues. "I read a novel once made up entirely of conversation. Two men talking in a jail cell. Or between separate cells. I don't think they could see each other. Somehow the one prisoner took care of the other by telling him stories. Scheherazade. To keep him alive. Keep his spirits up. One man was very sick, and one was gay. I can't remember if the sick one was also the gay one, but I think not. No, the gay one was the caretaker. I'm almost sure of it, because, I hate to admit this—it was 1974 or something—it was the first time I had the thought 'Oh, gays are just like us!' Horrible, eh? You don't even know sometimes how deep your prejudice goes until you react like that.

"My son's gay. Though he's never bothered to mention it to me or his father. You're not gay, are you?"

"I don't think so."

"You strike me as—"

"Gay?" Jeff guffaws in surprise.

"As a caretaker."

"Tell my wife. I take care of all the wrong people, according to her."

"She feels neglected?"

"I've done some bad things."

"We all make mistakes."

"Oh yes, some bad ones."

"Can you tell me?"

Jeff blinks. He's never met one like this. Sometimes they are angry; sometimes they want to hold his hand and pray. "My wife had a miscarriage."

"I'm sorry. It happens. This was *your* fault?"

"I couldn't be there." He coughs, shifts in his seat, and at that moment his pager starts to vibrate on his hip like a June bug flipped on its back. He slips off the pager, checks the number. Shit. Herman Byer. Stephanie at the office must have given out the number. "Excuse me," he says. "I've got to make a call."

"Of course. Make a call. Do you need my permission?"

Jeff colors for a moment. "I'll just use my cell. Keep the lines open."

Susan nods. "Take it in the bedroom. More privacy."

Heading upstairs, Jeff feels his stomach twist with dread. This on top of everything. He takes out his phone, dials. Where he's standing in Susan's room, he can touch the slanted ceiling with the tip of his middle finger. The ring stops.

"Left you a message this morning. Don't know if you heard." Herman Byer's voice is oatmeal thick with phlegm and tobacco, but Jeff has no trouble understanding. He grew up with these voices, these accents. The monosyllabic farmers suited like soldiers in their drab coveralls. He'd know the smell of this man, too, if he were standing beside him in his frozen barnyard, or sitting on a nearby stool at the diner counter. These farmers smelled of cow shit, of a morning spent wallowing in it until the smell meant nothing to them.

"I heard, all right. What happened?"

"Weren't nothing particular," the boy's grandfather says in the same sludgy way. "He was a good boy."

Like he's already dead.

"His grandmaw don't like 'im, that's all. Don't sleep good when he's here."

"Corey's giving you trouble?" Jeff can hear the man's drawn breath and the evaluating of his thoughts. For honesty, perhaps.

"Can't say that."

"He's doing okay in school?"

"Gets by, I guess."

Jeff breathes deeply himself now, trying to expel through his nose the air he's suddenly filled with. "You and your wife know what it means for Corey if you can't keep him? Even acquitted, it's nearly impossible to place a juvie with a record like his."

The grandfather has the good enough sense to be silent for a moment, though Jeff can hear a woman in the background, higher pitched, wanting to know what's been said, and even with the man covering the receiver, he can hear the relayed "Hush up."

"Can't they find him a home?" the grandfather asks.

"I wish. Bloomville's more likely. He's young, but that's where they're going to send him. Only place can't say no. Mr. Byer, your boy—"

"It's my son's kid. Don't ask me where he is."

Jeff clears his throat. "Better off locking Corey in a room and throwing away the key than sending him up to Bloomville. He'd be better off if you shoot him. Rough place, Bloomville. Very rough. And be honest with what you're telling me—"

The grandfather grunts low, cutting him off, and Jeff thinks for a moment he must be talking to an animal, not a human.

"She won't have him. Can't sleep."

Take a goddamn pill. "Can I talk to Mrs. Byer? I might be able to explain—"

Muffled voices then, and before Corey's grandfather gets back, Jeff already can figure the answer.

"Oh here," the grandfather says, "just talk."

"Mrs. Byer?" Her breath on the other end of the line sounds like rushing water.

"We don't want him and we don't plan to keep him. You take him or I call the police."

"That fire was an accident, Mrs. Byer. You heard the judge say so." *You heard it, but of course, you didn't believe it.*

"Ain't going to be any more accidents."

"You're scared." The instant the words are out Jeff knows he's made a mistake.

"The boy's not right. Don't speak a damn word, can't tell what he's thinking. I got responsibility to my husband, my animals. They come first. You may not like it, but that's the way it is."

That's the way it is. Adults first, kids last. Lambs to the slaughter. Jeff closes his cell phone, stuffs his knuckles in his mouth and bites hard to keep from screaming. He'd like to kick something. Just kick the shit out of something. Anything. Ram right through this plasterboard, the flimsy-looking doors on Susan's wardrobe, the paned glass window, six on six. He'd like to roar the goddamn roof off. Everything's the way it is—Leanne's gone; Corey's doomed; Christopher's lying stone dead beneath a veil of snow.

That's the way it is, his father used to say as he opened his buck, running his blade round the butt hole, through the pelvis, and up to the rib cage while he, Jeff, stood watching, feeling the edge of the blade sink deep, feeling a line of pain in his own body from the base of his ribs to the pit of his belly. With one gloved hand, his father reached up inside the slit cavity, loosened the lungs, cut the esophagus, and tugged until a stillborn mess of bloody organs came sliding out, spilling blood into the snow.

Ripped *him* open, the day his father left.

Jeff doesn't hear the door open, doesn't hear someone come in. Then Susan is there beside him on the edge of the bed.

"Tell me, Jeff. What's this all about?"

He presses his thumb and forefinger against his eyelids to keep them sealed. "It's fucked up. Incredibly fucked up."

"It is, isn't it? So tell me."

Leanne lost her job at the Quickway not long after Jeff took her in. Nailed for sneaking what she no longer had to sneak. Tim, the manager, had been watching her in the silver mirror that tilted the aisles and made the world bulge. *Warn't three strikes*, he told her. *Just one.*

"Maybe if I'd slept with him—" Leanne stamped out her cigarette and glared at Jeff.

A *warning.* He had fixed them both soup, tomato soup, made with milk the way she said she liked it, though he preferred water, and as he carried their bowls to the table, he was conscious of her gaze on him, her eyes slitted as if to size up her prey.

He wasn't bad-looking, he knew, except for his strange legs. He wobbled from time to time on them like they were going to break. A stumble out of no place like a horse too tense in its step. And sure enough, with her eyes on him, and her challenge still cracking in the air, he felt his knee lock. The orange soup spilled over his knuckles, burning them, but he managed to hold on to the bowls long enough to set them on the table.

Then he fetched a rag from the sink, apologizing as he wiped up the splotches of tomato soup on the table and swiped the rim of her bowl. Apologizing for his clumsiness. Apologizing to her who'd done nothing, nothing for him, but sleep on his couch, eat his soup and coffee and bread. Put a few dollars in a cup for rent, for heat, just a few since she'd lost her job. She said she would look for another. Fine, he said. He wasn't keeping tabs.

One night, a couple weeks later, Leanne reached across the

table, grabbed his wrist. "Let's do it," she said. He thought he might be dreaming. He really thought he might.

He'd never had a true love. Not by a long shot. He'd had crushes since he was a young boy. He was victim of a thousand sloppy love notes: his to the pursued. As a boy, the replies he got were giggles and taunts. Later on, guilty confessions, apologies—when he went to war, when he came back—from those girls who had spurned him for other men, men they regretted but never seemed to leave.

He'd more or less resigned himself—she'll find me, he thought. A driver with a flat tire, a fire widow, someone's sister, someone new to town—then he'd chastise himself for the dream of exploiting someone's distress. Why did he think only a woman in distress would find a need for him?

He wasn't a virgin, but he'd never slept with a woman like Leanne.

In the morning, Leanne told him that he was better in bed than she'd thought he'd be. More tender, more skilled than anyone she'd yet been with. His knees had scared her, though, when she'd discovered how swollen they were, like the knotted swellings in the bark of the old apple trees behind her parents' trailer. She'd liked the rest of his body, though. So strong. So muscled and thick. Hard but not unkind.

She'd been fucked every which way, she told him. Been shoved and tied and ordered. With those men, she'd freeze herself up. Make believe she was a hunk of granite older than Mars. But with him, she felt different, she said. Like caramel. Like a sheet of caramel wrapped around a hard apple. Her special treat, she said. When her father took her to the fair.

But making love to Leanne, Jeff discovered, was like walking a mine field. Unexpected explosions at every turn. Once he began lapping at her nipples, shifting teat to teat like a greedy kitten, when out of the blue a burst of pain in his groin and his shoulders shoved hard. He froze, terrified, going limp. "I ain't your fucking mother," she said.

On other nights, she covered his body with kisses, his aching knees, his stiff hip, the shiny patches of road rash where the pigment had burned away and a new skin formed in its place, translucent as black ice. He was a map of 'Nam, he told her. A formed topo map, each puckered ridge of scar tissue contained a memory of pain: winged darts of shrapnel from an exploded tank; burns from a land mine that took his comrade's life. When she kissed those elevated places, they tingled, sensation building on sensation until he cried out in ecstasy and grief.

Leanne tossed and muttered in her sleep, grinding her teeth like a nervous horse. Her dreams, she told him, were booby-trapped. So were his. But for a long time after Leanne started sharing his bed, his dreams quieted as he tended to hers.

After the Quickway, Leanne got a job at a day care run out of a friend's house. She loved the kids. She was happy. He noticed little changes—she wasn't smoking as much, because it wasn't permitted at work; she wore her hair back or up and stopped wearing hoops and dangling earrings. On weekends, she liked to go to yard sales, scouting for toys and puzzles and books for "her kids." She didn't seem to mind so much his being away on calls.

Then one night she dropped a bombshell. She wanted to get married, she said, 'cause all the little kids asked. And she thought she should set an example, seeing as none of their mothers were.

He was fine with that, he told her. They could get married as soon as she wanted. Leanne wanted right away. No wedding or party. Just the two of them at the county office, then a night in a motel with a Jacuzzi and a king-sized bed.

And she had a funny idea. The wedding cake would be a gingerbread house. She'd bake it herself and load it with candy—like the gingerbread house she'd always dreamed of eating—she'd share it with the kids.

No problem. Done deal.

He rode a Harley in those days. His wedding present to Leanne was a black leather jacket, one she'd wanted, fringe hanging from the seams of the sleeves and across the back and chest. He liked watching the fringe shimmy with her gestures, a hundred flitting birds lifting, sinking.

A week later they stood inside the county courthouse, an old redbrick building trimmed in white bric-a-brac. The clerk, sitting behind a wooden grille, pushed papers at them across a marble lip. The building had once been a bank. It felt like a bank. High ceilings, marble floor, and a mural that ran the length of the wall which showed two Indians holding dead turkeys by their scrawny necks as they greeted one massive Pilgrim.

Jeff and Leanne filled out the forms, then stepped back to the clerk's window to return them. He was not one for public displays of affection, but he could not stop himself from flinging an arm around her neck and pulling her toward him in the crook of his elbow. Beneath his arm, he felt the slippery smoothness of Leanne's jacket like a second, impenetrable skin, he felt her muscles expand as she turned to kiss him, hard. *It's going to be all right*, he heard himself purr. *All right.*

The blood work was in order. Everything was in order. He had not forgotten her ring or she, his. Two plain gold bands with the date inscribed on the inner surface. He slipped her ring over her unpainted nail, her narrow finger; she slipped the ring over his.

"Are you going to keep your name?" the clerk asked, oblivious to the scene beyond her grille.

"Hell no," Leanne said. "Nothing about my name I'd want to keep."

Then a second bombshell. Leanne was pregnant. She was eighteen, legally married. He was, he realized, happy. Leanne seemed happy, too, Jeff thought. Despite the rough first trimester when even the sight of food sent her running to the toilet.

After that, though, she ate like a horse. She liked strawberry ice cream; hot dogs with ketchup and relish; bear claw pastries from her old place of employment—her old boss, perhaps feeling sorry, gave them to her free.

Leanne grew large. Not just with the baby, but with all the fat she was putting on. The doctor told her to slow down. You're risking diabetes, he said. High blood pressure.

Still, she ate. It was giving up the cigarettes, she said. It was having nothing to do once the doctor said she had to stay in bed to keep the placenta intact.

One day Leanne and Jeff went to the doctor, who hooked his stethoscope into his ears and turned the monitor up loud. In the past when Jeff had heard the *whoom whoom* of the baby's heartbeat, he'd thought of it as a signal from outer space, a longed-for sign of life from a distant planet.

This time, he and Leanne watched the doctor frown and sigh as he removed the scope from his ears and hooked it to theirs, an earpiece for each. The shared stethoscope clamped them together, his ear to her ear, his cheek to hers. They'd never gone on a vacation together, never gone anywhere, but here they were standing on a wind-torn shore, the monitor roaring at them like an angry surf.

The doctor was tall and thin with curly hair and a beard. His wrists looked kind, Jeff thought. And he said the right things, how sad it was, how disappointing, how it was nobody's fault the baby had been lost. But they had to make a decision now, he told them. The baby was stillborn.

"Still not born," Jeff corrected him.

The doctor frowned. "That, too."

Leanne began to sob. Jeff moved to put his arms around her shoulders, but she stayed curled. He wanted to sob with her, but he could not. Though his insides heaved with sadness, he remained sealed against the battering sea. Later he blamed this on his training, that it had been drummed into him to keep a clear head when others were losing theirs.

The doctor told them that they had some choices: he could induce labor today and that would relieve them of the nightmare in a couple of hours. They could schedule a C-section. Or they could wait to see if labor came on sometime in the next two weeks. The last would give Leanne the best chance of giving birth again.

"Think about it," the doctor said. "Call me when you decide."

That afternoon, Leanne took to her bed. He, to the Naugahyde sofa that smelled of stale beer. Lying on that sofa, he stared up at the squares of pocked ceiling tile and thought of every search he'd ever led—searches for the addled, for the insane, searches for the very young and very old, searches for runaways, and walkaways, and countless drunks, and he wanted to tell Leanne the one thing he'd learned from all of them, the one thing he cleaved to that kept him on track: the point of departure is the point of hope. You can't give up.

In the bedroom, she was lying on her side, her face turned to the wall, her hair loosed in a heavy mass around her shoulders. She was hidden beneath it in a way that made him think of an animal hidden in its den of needles. Asleep? Faking? He stood as still as he might in the woods and sure enough, after a time he saw her shoulder hitch, and heard a noise that sounded like a child's hiccough, only deeper. Who was she hiding from? Him, of course. All at once they were strangers again, the way they had begun.

When Leanne went into labor, Jeff was on a rescue. It was late October, a week after Leanne had decided to wait it out. A father and his eleven-year-old son were missing. They'd gone out orienteering for a day on state land, and when they didn't appear at dinner, the wife called the police.

When the call came in, Leanne told him not to go.

He thought she was being selfish. There had been nothing unusual that morning except a few freckles of blood in Leanne's underwear and on her sheets. She'd be all right, he said. Nothing was going to happen without daddy there. Later he'd wonder why he'd been stupid enough to say that.

He found Leanne asleep around midnight in a hospital bed in the maternity ward. Some blessed angel had given her a private room, but that was all the angel had given. A nurse wearing a shirt plastered with smiling teddies stopped by. Leanne had been brave, she told him. "But she was calling for you, poor girl. She definitely wanted you."

For hours, he sat in a chair beside the bed and thought of nothing but his own failure. At dawn another nurse came by. He had been certain Leanne was still sleeping deeply, but when she lifted Leanne's wrist to check her pulse, her eyelids opened instantly like a cat's, then sank like what she'd seen wasn't worth waking for. She had left him; he knew that. Their baby had been born still, and the small blue spark of her love for him had turned cold.

"How long ago did this happen?"

"A few years."

"She still hasn't forgiven you?"

"No."

"She's still young."

Jeff nods. "She is."

"You are, too."

Jeff coughs.

"Forty."

"Add nine."

"This is silly. You're young enough."

"You're ten years younger than your husband?"

"Twelve."

"My wife's a bit younger, too."

Susan nods. "Never seemed a problem when we met."

"When was that?"

"Oh, about thirty years ago, at a football game; we left early and walked along the Hudson River; ended up at an Irish bar. He was a builder; I was a grad student. He promised he'd build a lab for me someday."

"Did he?"

"Wasn't necessary. I was hired right out of school. But it was a nice thought. I'd never met anyone as thoughtful in my whole life."

"I met my wife in a bar, too. Not quite the same, though. More like twenty years on us. Twenty years' difference."

"Basin and range."

"What's that?"

"A geological formation. You see it out West. A steep ridge, followed by a long flat valley, another ridge, another valley."

"That's what it was like. A big drop in altitude."

"Christopher and I used to think that 'basin and range' was the perfect metaphor for aging. The elevations marked our new decades, and we swore the view was better from the top. But the truth is you can't ignore the descent."

Jeff bows his head, looking down at his interlocking knuckles. "She's got a friend."

"Ah."

"Left me for him last night."

"I'm sorry."

"It's not your fault."

Susan closes her eyes. "I'm sorry your wife can't love you, because you obviously love her. We were like that. Christopher and I. For years. But I made the mistakes, not him."

They are still seated shoulder to shoulder on the edge of the wide bed. And he can't help himself from turning toward her, seeking her face. "Like what?"

Susan blinks hard and Jeff finds himself locked in the gaze of those translucent eyes. "I lived a secret life."

"A 'secret life'?"

"The kind of life Leanne's living now. Apart from you. Apart from anyone, really. I thought I was the only person in the world." Strange, how she sees it now, not as a betrayal, not as anything personal, but as the experience of having felt intensely alive.

"You loved your husband?"

Susan frowns and her gaze drops as she soothes the middle knuckle of her left hand with the thumb and middle finger of her right. Then she looks up at him, her eyes lit with triumph. "We got lost together once in a rain forest. On an island. We were totally and completely lost, but we survived."

Eighteen

The searchers have gone up and down the main roads and the back roads. They have covered the meadows, acres of sheared stubble, cradling frozen springs, mud puddles, dried flops. There are plenty of corpses—deer and porcupine and rabbit and mole. There are scraps of blue flannel, but Christopher wasn't wearing blue flannel; there is a boot without laces, the sole arced in an impossible U; there are pages of newspaper and ancient condoms—a whole cache of them beside a frozen blanket—but given the task and the weather, no one has the wherewithal to crack the obvious jokes.

Two men develop frostbite on their cheeks. The sun is starting to go down. Nothing spectacular: the slow intrusion of indigo and eggplant; the slow peeling back of day into night.

There is a moon. Half of one. And a thin coating of snow—enough to create a reflection, to cast shadows in the woods. But Jeff says they will not search past dark. Too dangerous. Too cold. There aren't enough flashlights.

NINETEEN

JEFF TURNS THE WHEEL HARD INTO THE DRIVEWAY, HALF expecting lights, half expecting to see Leanne's Skylark or Jimmy's van, but the driveway's empty. The small house a black rock against the deep navy sky.

He pushes open the door, but is reluctant to turn on the lights. It feels all of a sudden like his home has been stolen from him. When last he lived here, a year ago this morning, he was papa bear, now he's Goldilocks. Yet as far as he can tell, nothing has changed since he left. Toast crumbs on his plate, the shiny lid of yogurt lying grimed side up on the kitchen table. What he's looking for are signs of her, of Leanne. Has she been here? Did she stop home? Is it still her home?

All day time has been linear; they go forward, they search, they find, and they rescue. But now as Jeff walks into the bedroom, time has circled back, the darkness, the smell of his old sweat and hers, the smell of burned wood and rust, the smell of abandoned fire. Jeff lifts the lid off the porthole on the top of the stove and peers in at the bed of ash, then slides it back. It's an old stove, no fancy baffles, no window glass, nothing kind or efficient about it. But good enough to heat this small house. Safe enough.

He cleans it himself. It's a bitch to get started, though, and right now he'd rather roll himself in blankets without taking off his clothes. He just wants to sleep.

The telephone jangles Jeff awake. No matter how tired he is, he sleeps lightly, like the mother of a newborn, a line left open to the waking world.

Then the cold black mobile is in his hand and Leanne's voice rushes into his ear as though she never doubted she'd reach him.

Usually people aren't allowed back where the jail is, but Wiltsie is manning the desk, and with one glance at the monitor he buzzes Jeff through. No wave or greeting of any kind. Jeff is grateful Wiltsie isn't going to make him go through all that shit. He's too tired, too fucking tired for all of that.

The corridor is narrow with white cinder-block walls and a smooth gray floor. A single fluorescent tube snakes along the high ceiling. Tonight Jeff notices how the hallway shunts you to the jail as if it were designed with calming influences in mind like the chutes that steer cattle to the slaughterhouse.

Leanne's not been slaughtered. She's very much alive, sitting on a wooden bench behind cream-colored bars, feet bare, hair twisted through its own strands to hold it in a loose bun at her neck. The cell looks to Jeff like a giant dog crate. A cage in a zoo. See our exotic specimen: our rare find. A *dangerous* woman. A repeat DWI.

Without a word, he pulls out a pack of cigarettes from his jacket pocket, her brand, and drops them through the slotlike opening in the front of the cell.

Leanne remains seated. She reminds him, not for the first

time, of a mare he had as a boy, a bony roan who parked herself in a boggy corner of the field among burdock and thorn apple and refused to be caught. Day after day she stood knee deep in the mud where the stream overflowed its banks. Her legs grew scaly with rot and her hooves stank of thrush, but she didn't care. No matter how good the treat he offered her, she ignored it and him. Being untouchable is what she lived for.

"Leanne. C'mon."

Silence.

Even though Leanne is in full view, Jeff has the feeling she is hiding. "What happened?"

Leanne shrugs. "Had a few drinks; hit a patch of black ice—"

For a moment he imagines it: the feel of flying, skidding, and not knowing how it will end. "Jimmy was with you." He had picked this up off the radio.

"Yeah."

The jail is quiet tonight. The adjacent cell stands empty, its door slightly ajar. Jeff steps back. The cell looks peaceful. The wide wooden bench; the shiny gray floor. He could use a night in a cell, he thinks. A day and night of quiet and security. He should lock himself in. Lock himself next to her and maybe after a day or a week or a month, Leanne would tap to him against their mutual wall.

He shoves his hand in his pants pocket this time, and pulls out a lighter. "Can't drop this."

In a flash, Leanne's up, grabbing the lighter from between the bars, sweeping the cigarettes from the floor. She wheels back to her bench with her prizes like a wily crow. But all of a sudden the lighter slips through her fingers, skittering along the cell floor and back through the bars like a boomerang to rest an inch or so beyond the toe of Jeff's boot.

They both freeze. Then Jeff stoops to pick up the lighter.

Holding it at arm's length, he contemplates it in his open palm like a curious artifact.

"Don't be a prick," Leanne says.

He steps away from the cell, flicks on the lighter. This must be how a lion tamer feels, he thinks. Someone performing on the edge.

"Give it." Leanne's face presses against the bars.

"What's the magic word?"

"Fuck you."

Jeff shakes his head. The cigarette wags between her lips like a catbird's tail. He brings the flame near the tip, watching her eyes hood and her nostrils flare as she anticipates the pleasure of the inhale. "Leanne. Can't we stop? Please? I want to. I want to stop and be who we really are."

He hadn't planned to say this, not any of it. He'd wanted to punish her, to be as cruel as he possibly could. But then it seemed like pretend, so much tedious pretend.

When he'd stepped into her hospital room that night, a room not much bigger than this one, she was not alone. A nurse in a white dress, white shoes sat tight as a nun on a chair beside the bed. On Leanne's chest lay a papoose of draped white flannel, and even though he knew, even though he'd been told his son would be born dead, his heart leaped, no tore, through his chest and his lungs released in a cry of hope.

Leanne did not awake. A sedative had hammered her into sleep.

The nurse stood up. It was his turn, she said. His turn to hold the huddled object they called his son.

Leanne drags on her cigarette, exhaling two streams of smoke through her nostrils like a doe on a winter's night. "Did he make it?"

" 'He'?" Christopher? The baby who never had a chance?

"Jimmy." She casts her gaze down, her toe tracing an arc on the gray enamel floor. Jeff clears his throat, and it is as if he is looking into a tunnel with only a bead of flame in its depths. He has seen Leanne angry; he has seen her frozen with grief; but he has never seen her like this: scared. He's jealous, and also somehow humbled. It's the kind of humble he feels looking through crosshairs at the brow of a stag, erect, motionless, yet ready to spring away. No matter how well he thinks he knows this woman, he doesn't.

"Jimmy's okay," he says. "He lived."

TWENTY

ONCE HE ASKED HIS MOM WHY THE SKY WAS BLUE AND SHE looked at him funny and said, "To make the clouds look white, stupid."

But that didn't seem right, so he asked Lance and he said, "Spray paint."

He thought it might be like an egg, like a robin's egg shell turned inside out, and when you got up there you cracked right through. Astronauts got past the blue but how did you get past the black and what color was that? It didn't seem like there was God or even a place called heaven like the minister who did the funeral for Lance said. He couldn't see Lance as an angel, the way the minister said. He might even be in hell, though it was bad to think so. Something told him Lance would like that better. He was a devil, their mother used to say. His middle name was Trouble. But really it was his first name, too. What they should have called him.

Lance liked to be in trouble; he liked to start stuff. Lance was always getting sent to the principal, sent home. Everybody was scared of Lance because he wasn't scared of anything. He was scared of Lance, too, because he did stuff everybody else was scared to do. He jumped off the railroad tracks over the creek; he walked them, too. On his first day of seventh grade, he got caught drawing cartoons of the teacher rolled over by a truck. Corey didn't get why Lance had Mrs. Bernard rolled over with blood spurting out of her side and out of her head and a bubble screaming, *"Help! Help!"* Mrs. Bernard was an old lady and she didn't hear too good, but instead of getting crabby about it, she almost always laughed. Mrs. Bernard was the nicest teacher in the school.

Lance did other stuff, too. Plugging toilets up with toilet paper in the boys' room; lighting things on fire—crickets and dead flies; making cannons out of sawed-off soda cans stuffed with rags soaked in gasoline. He was always looking for stuff to burn. "Let's see what this's like; let's see how that goes." He liked to set plastic soldiers on fire. Watching their faces melt, he'd make his voice go high and whiny as a girl's: "I'm dying, I'm dying."

Flicka the Bic.

But where was Lancie now? he wondered. Was he completely gone? He wondered this all the time. The worms crawl in, the worms crawl out. But after the house burned down there was nothing left of his brother to crawl out of. It might be better that way. Nobody wanted worms in them.

Once his grandmother had read him a Bible story about two brothers and one brother was really liked by everybody, especially his mother, even though he wasn't so hot, and the other wasn't liked by anyone except his father. But the one who wasn't liked was the good boy. He was the boy who worked really hard and liked animals, but the other boy was the tricky one and he dressed himself in fur to be like his animal brother to trick the father and the father believed him and blessed him before he died and the good boy who worked hard and loved animals had to go away.

At the end of the story his grandmother looked at him. "Which boy are you?" she asked, and he was confused because he was both boys, the boy who loved animals and also the younger boy who put on fur. He could see himself putting on fur, wrapping himself in a bearskin or the hide of a horse. He thought that was an idea, a trick he could play on his brother.

"Which are you?" she asked again.

"Don't know."

That was when he talked. Not much, but he did talk. Listened, too. Listened to all the lies his brother told him—that their dad had murdered somebody once; that their mother was a whore. He wanted to beat Lance up; he wanted to shut him up, stuff his mouth up like Lance stuffed those toilets. He put his hands over his ears, but Lance pulled them down. "Only words, asshole," his brother said. Only words, but each sank into him with its poisoned tip.

A lot of people thought they didn't have a father. They had a father. Everybody did. He and Lance had the same father, Bob, but Justin, the baby, had a different one. He never knew his name. Bob was his grandfather's son, but he didn't know where he went same as everybody else.

When his dad left, he was too scared to ask where he'd gone, when he was coming back, but Lance wasn't. He went right up to their mother and he sounded mad like it was her fault, but even Lance was scared a bit, he knew this, because he was twitching his right wrist, flicking it, flicking it, trying to shoo a fly that wasn't there.

Don't blame me, his mother said. Not my fault. No way to

make a living up here no more; drinking too much. But he knew what it really was: it was him. He stressed his father; he stressed everybody even though it was Lance who always done the bad stuff; it was him who drove everybody apart.

The thing he remembered most about his father was his arms. Every bit had muscle. They bulged up and down. He liked to clench his fist to show him the hard hill: "Squeeze it, pinch it, c'mon, nothing can hurt."

Lance was the first to try it. He gave it everything, squeezing their father's muscle with both hands, making sure his nails dug in.

Watching, he expected their father to get mad; to drop Lance right there. But he didn't. The redder Lance got, the more their father laughed. "Now my stomach," he said. He was wearing a white shirt with tiny ribs running down the front, no sleeves. His chest was pushed out, but his belly made a scooped cave. "Hit me. Hit me hard as you can."

Lance pushed him forward. He didn't look up, just touched the white T-shirt with a couple of light knocks. The T-shirt felt soft where it grazed his knuckles.

"Harder," his father said. "Shit."

He tried again. This time he felt the muscle underneath. It felt like rock. But he couldn't punch any harder. He was too scared. It seemed like a stupid thing to do. It seemed like asking for it.

Then Lance stepped up. He shoved his fist hard into the cave. His father's mouth flattened for a second, then came up a smile, and Lance backed off, looking puzzled at the pain in his knuckles.

"Hit me again," his father said, but Lance shook his head. His knuckles still hurt.

Later Lance told him their father was made of steel—at least part of him. He had a metal plate where his stomach should be. Their father was like Superman, he said. If anyone jumped him or stabbed him, he'd be okay. But if they set him on fire, he'd burn.

Part II
Saturday

Twenty-one

EVERY SATURDAY MORNING COREY AND HIS GRANDFATHER went to the diner. Corey did not like going to the diner with his grandfather. The whole small room was filled with men in bulging jackets and shit-smeared boots, backs bowed over their coffee cups. When the door jingled, their heads turned, and they nodded. They nodded at his grandfather, but not at him, him they passed over like a post. They never spoke to him. They knew all about him, but never spoke.

Today the talk in the diner was all of the man who was missing. He was from the city, lived up the road, but no one knew him or his wife. They didn't farm. They didn't visit the diner. In the paper, the wife of the missing man was quoted: "Some days he's almost normal, some days disoriented. It's unfortunate." Twenty minutes after her husband was gone, she went looking, but couldn't catch up.

Doreen, the waitress and also the owner's wife, raised the pot she already held in her hand. "More coffee, anyone?" she asked, though the men's answers were always the same. "You?" She looked at him.

His grandfather tilted his head at him. "Give him milk if that's what he wants." He did.

No one in that room except his grandfather had ever heard his voice. His voice slept and slept inside his chest, and he wasn't sure now if he even remembered anymore how to wake it up.

On his first morning on the farm, Corey awoke in a sweat. Flames blazed across the sky, redder than anything he'd ever seen, redder than a house on fire. A red so bright the trees were stripped bare, black limbs against scarlet, and he screamed, pounding down the attic stairs, not bothering with coat or shoes.

"Fire!" he cried. This time he got it right.

His grandfather sat up in bed, shaking his gray head like a waking bear, but his grandmother leaped up and grabbed his arms. "I don't smell smoke."

Then his grandfather was up, too, and pushing them toward the stairs and down the stairs and out the front door.

There they saw—and he saw—the fire in the woods—the fire behind the woods—the sunrise, torching the eastern sky.

"You little asshole," his grandfather said. His cheek was sore for hours where he slapped him. He did not speak to his grandparents much again.

He and his grandfather sat at the curve in the counter next to the bathroom. That was his grandfather's place, where you had to pretend you couldn't hear the sound of someone crapping behind the thin wall or smell the putrid air that escaped when the door opened.

His grandfather picked up the paper on the counter, held it wide enough that the boy could see, too. The picture in the paper didn't look anything like the man he found yesterday in the woods. This man was smiling, his eyes crinkled with a joke. And his hair was combed neat to one side and his shirt was open. But right away the boy knew this man was his man. He could tell by the set of his nose, the long curve of his jaw. And he felt proud for some reason. Excited and proud like he'd done something right, not touching him, not telling his secret.

"Well, why in heck didn't she go after him?" his grandfather said, shutting the paper, pushing out his cup for Doreen.

The boy watched her pour his grandfather's warm-up like she was watering the geranium that sat inside the window in a box.

"They're fast," she said. "And sneaky. I know. Worked in a nursing home once. Like herding sheep."

"Bring in the dogs then," his grandfather said.

The folded paper lay in front of the boy like a dog resting on its side. He wanted to open it; he wanted to look at the picture of the man again, the lost sheep, but he didn't dare. His story had been in the paper, too. They had got it all wrong. Names and spelling and other stuff. They had made his aunt his grandma and his uncle his father. He had not read the story himself, but he'd been told that his mother was angry that they'd got it all wrong.

No one from the paper had asked him how it happened. An act of God, they wrote. A boy thing. Horsing around with his brother. But his brother was asleep.

If the reporter had asked him how it happened he would not have known what to say. Leaves he ignited with a magnifying glass he took from school; if he held the glass just so, the white circle grew brighter and brighter until it gave way to smoke then fire, nothing so big he couldn't stomp it with his boot.

But the paper towel when he lit it turned into a bouquet of flame and flew away. The curtain went up like magic and a nightmare. In seconds it was a blaze, a mane of yellow flames. Beautiful, but scary.

He ran into the hallway, expecting to find his aunt and uncle, and down the stairs; he was screaming their names, screaming his way all the way outside. Only after he ran did he remember his brother, snoring on the bed. His brother slept like lead, while he slept restlessly like feathers never settling. Beneath his brother's bed was the box of lighters—all the colors of the rainbow exploding in flame.

He did not know what happened when you burned and he was scared to know. He had gotten burned, but not a lot compared with his aunt and uncle. He had been in the hospital, too, but on another floor. His room was decorated with Mario posters and Star Wars and Harry Potter. His bed was private, surrounded with bars like a crib, but he didn't mind. He had his own TV and video games. He had a bell he could ring if he got thirsty or scared. Whenever he rang it, a nurse came with a can of cold soda. "Lonely?" she asked, but he didn't have to answer.

What he was left with was patches, light against his darker skin. He was pinto now, his grandfather said. Pinto. Like a horse.

"Who's doing the looking?" his grandfather asked Doreen.

"Most of the guys," Louie jumped in. "Want to come?" Louie drove the cattle truck and looked like a steer, with his big square head and wide-spaced eyes. He held his check and his money out to Doreen, getting up to go.

"Bad hip," his grandfather grunted, as if Louie didn't know. His grandfather flipped pancakes for the firehouse breakfasts and fashioned meatballs with his bare hands for the dinners. But he never went out with the men. "Take him," his grandfather said, nodding his way.

"Him?" Louie cut his sly eyes at the boy and shook his head.

"Can't blame you," his grandfather said. "Screw came loose on this one. Ain't no one can tighten it."

His grandfather slapped a couple of dollars on the check Doreen slipped under the rim of his saucer. Then he shoved his hand in his front pocket and added a bit of change. Grunting, he patted the brim of his cap and came off his stool. "You coming?"

he said. Corey nodded. "Thought so. We got work to do today. We ain't like those sons of bitches take the day to go hunting."

In the truck, his grandfather wasn't finished with the topic. "You know why they do it, don't you? Want to be heroes every one of them. Go straight to heaven if you save a man's life."

What if you find them dead? What if you already killed somebody?

TWENTY-TWO

SUSAN AWAKES WITH A START, HER HEART SEEMING TO WELL IN her chest, an inflated drum. In her dream, the house, not this house, was shaking, the ancient walls shifting and crumbling, and a terrible sound, a w*homp, whomp, whomp* like boulders dropping one on top of another drowned out her cries for help. "Shit," she says, sitting up quickly, covering her ears. The noise is real.

At the window, she tugs the blinds, tries to clear her head. Outside the window the search helicopter hovers, monstrous, confused.

She leaves the window, staggers back to her bed. The helicopter. But it's too late to detect body heat. Surely it's too late. Last night the possibilities of how Christopher might still be alive spun through her head like tigers running themselves into butter: a snow cave; a neighbor's shed or barn; a trucker's cab; a stranger's lift. She had left word with Lieutenant Higgs to call her no matter what time of the night if he got any word. But there had been no word.

She had thought of calling Peter then. She had picked up the telephone; she had dialed. It would take a while to get through, a series of clicks and eerie whistles as if to prove that the connection flew outside of the stratosphere and back. As she waited, she tried to steady her breathing, tried to think of how to tell Peter of her near certainty that his father was dead. She found it was like scrambling a peak, the adrenaline of wanting to reach a summit made her mind come into focus, made her think, *Remember you're the mother*. But the summit was false. Peter did not pick up. Nor did the crazy answering machine with its inane message. After she placed the receiver back in its base, she stared at it for a moment as though it had betrayed her, and she thought of trying to reach Peter again, but now she wasn't certain of what she wanted to say.

Below, the searchers are already swarming. The mix of mustard-colored coats and EMT blue and the state troopers in their soft gray hats, their purple ties.

And she wants to break down, crying, shaking, but she tells herself that's not what's needed right now; she just can't fall apart.

The temperature is in the teens; it is almost ten o'clock. The sky is blue. Susan's living room window has become her widow's walk. From here, she watches Jeff veer off from the others to make his way to her door. Even with those stiff knees, he moves more quickly than other men, she thinks. As if to prove something.

The doorbell chimes. She is ready for him, dressed sensibly in flannel-lined trousers, a wool sweater. "Well," she says. "The helicopter."

"Yeah." He is shaking his head, looking at the floor, not at her. His skin looks gray. *Hard to face the survivors*, she hears him thinking. "Not a lot of news," Jeff says.

Even though she thought she was prepared for this, his words flood her with despair, the despair he told her not to give in to. "What happens now?"

Jeff silences her with a finger. His radio is squawking. Something incomprehensible to her, but he appears transfixed. "K-9's on the way with dogs."

"Dogs? Isn't it too late?"

Jeff shakes his head. "I know, but Chief says dogs."

Susan nods. It's out of her hands, it really is; why does she bother to say anything? "What will you need?"

"Dirty socks, dirty shorts. Anything that's got his scent. I'll bring bags and gloves—you don't want to touch anything."

"Of course not." Years of training in the lab—you don't contaminate anything with your bare hands. "But listen, Jeff, you told me no dogs, now there are dogs, and this morning there's a goddamn helicopter that should have been here yesterday." Her voice is rising to a shout. "And so many fucking people out there—forget finding a scent. I want an accurate assessment of what's going on."

Jeff looks at her. His cheeks are red now; his eyes glassy. It strikes Susan that he might be genuinely sick. "I told you to keep up the hope."

The hope. What hope? "Then it's recovery." Even as she says this, she would like to suck back the words.

Jeff grunts and sticks his hands in the pockets of his coat, which he never took off. His gaze burns a small hole in the floor, a gaze, Susan thinks, that feels like shame. *Did his wife return last night?*

Then his chin comes up, and he looks at her with those inscrutable eyes. "In my book, it's not recovery until the body's found."

As soon as she's given Jeff what he needs, she makes her way upstairs again, slides again into her bed. The light shifts. She should have closed the blinds. The light pushes in, making it difficult to breathe. Peter should be here. Peter, who just now might be sipping tea in a hut in Libreville. Peter. Her son. *Their* son. Why does she always think of him as hers? Peter. An image flashes in her mind of his sunburned neck, hair follicles raised white as gooseflesh when he scratches back there.

Will he come for the funeral? Will he if she asks? Nearly ten thousand dollars it will cost to get him home and a project interrupted. She won't ask.

It's not recovery until the body's found.

She knows; David Kappelman's body in a plain pine box, a slim loaf borne by black-coated men. Prayers flowed, unceasing, into her ears. She didn't understand a word of them, yet the melody conveyed what it had to: that the earth was crying—that sorrow was an ancient song. How can she believe that Christopher is dead? How can she really believe it? Believing is seeing.

Susan closes her eyes. She wants to pray, but she cannot. She does not know a single prayer, except a line from Wordsworth, a fragment plucked from a poem she must have been asked to memorize in school, but of which only these words remain: *"Rolled round in earth's diurnal course, / With rocks, and stones, and trees."* She thinks of Peter again, so far away, on another planet, it seems. But if he were here, he'd find his father. She's sure of it. He sensed where to find him before. Peter suggested to Susan that she tell the police to look for his dad in his studio. This is where they found him. She sees the scene again. She, sitting by the telephone, racked with panic; Peter like a snake appearing from out of nowhere.

TWENTY-THREE

PETER CAME TO VISIT SHORTLY AFTER THEY MOVED. THE FUND-ing for his expedition was in place; soon he would undertake a thousand-mile trek across uncharted lands from Gabon to the Ivory Coast, cataloguing every possible specimen of flora and fauna he could find. Miraculously, he'd gotten the okay from the sitting heads of state of the countries he'd be tromping through. Radio and television deals had been finalized. Only a few visa odds and ends remained to be sorted out. So he could visit them en route to the embassies in Washington, he said. The route bumped him far out of his way, but he was used to circuitous routes.

Susan was astonished, grateful, to be included in his itinerary. "You could fly up, you know," she said. "There's a small airstrip."

Peter had learned to pilot a plane since doing field work in Africa. He loved to fly.

"Good idea," Peter said. "Saves time." He was calling from New York, and he had a friend who could loan him a plane. "Believe it or not, I've got all kinds of money I don't need for getting around in the States. It's expedition money I'm still scram-bling for."

His voice had dropped when he was thirteen. She remembered the shock of it. The baby gone; a gear shifting. He had a beautiful baritone, a particularly resonant voice. He was a good public speaker for someone who spent such long stretches of time in near silence.

But he had confided to her that he hated that side of the job, those dues he had to pay to live the life he was passionately in love with. "I can talk to funders," he said. "And I'm glad I can do it well. But when I'm up there talking to a bunch of geographical systems geeks, I feel like an ape wearing a straitjacket. Can't breathe."

She'd listened sympathetically. A little over a year ago, she'd reached Peter on satellite phone to tell him about Christopher's dementia. He was just about to board a prop plane to track elephant herds across Ghana. After a pause, he started questioning her intensively; had they considered drug interaction? Hypoglycemia? Graves' disease? Yes, yes, and yes, she answered, but she was scribbling down his surmises, vowing to herself to pass them along to the doctor. He did not offer to fly home; she did not expect him to. Before he hung up, he said, "You can handle it, Mom. You've handled some pretty tough shit already. You're going to be okay." And that had left her so confused, aswoon with her son's estimation and dying to confess to him that she felt afraid.

"So it's a deal. I'll e-mail the coordinates for the airport. You call when you're taking off." Just then she noticed Christopher coming down the stairs, and she could feel her skin tighten over her cheekbones and her gut turn over. "Got to go, honey," she said. "Dad." She put down the telephone.

Christopher had made his way down the stairs. By himself. Gripping tightly to the banister as though the whole staircase might be the thrashing back of a dragon.

He was sweating. Gleaming moisture at his temples. Beneath his chin. Exertion? Fear? The meds?

"Christopher!" she said joyfully, crossing the room to join him. "Peter's coming to visit. Peter. Our son!"

He looked at her, nodding to acknowledge her mood, but clearly lost all the same.

"Peter," she said. "Peter Peter Peter." *Peter, peter, peter*, she thought. *The cardinal's song.*

Christopher shook his head. His nails gripped her arm as he caught on to it, a bird alighting. "Daddy," he said. "Daddy coming. My daddy."

Susan was delighted. *"You're* Daddy. *Peter's* your son. Here comes Peter."

"Peter Peter Peter," Christopher sang out. He seemed happy.

Peter was coming. She felt a bit like a war bride welcoming home the man she hadn't seen for years. But wasn't it the other way around? She and Christopher were the ones in the trench, ducking a thousand mortar rounds a day. How could she explain this to Peter? Should she even try?

She had been reading Peter's blog every day on the website of the scientific organization that was sponsoring his trek. His voice in these dispatches had taken on a manic tone that worried her. He was still in the process of hiring porters, getting permissions, coordinating food drops, and a million other details. One thousand miles he planned to go; no stopping him; a juggernaut fueled by God knows what.

Words of caution bubbled up in her. Ebola existed in that part of world. Hepatitis, AIDS, and mysterious illnesses simply known as "monkey fevers." Peter knew this, of course. Her warnings weren't worth a damn.

What she sent instead were encouraging words. Upbeat reports on Christopher. She found herself sounding like a young mother in these dispatches. She remembered writing notes like these to her parents, desperately waggling the baby genius's doings to gain their attention. What a waste. Her parents, though polite, though distantly fond, remained indifferent. It was exactly, she realized, how they had treated her.

When she was six, her parents sent her off to a boarding school in the country. A reasonable place, with reasonable teachers. No story of abuse here. She was an easy child, a docile child, easy to overlook, except for her brains. Which, her teachers informed her, were outstanding. She never really understood this. Tests never seemed to test anything. Facts about plants and animals and revolutions and kings, French tenses and equations both mathematical and chemical flowed into her brain and were easily netted—but what did all of that have to do with *intelligence*?

And then, mysteriously, she was summoned home to attend a private school nearby. Did this coincide with her mother's finally being granted tenure? With her father's being awarded the first of several prizes in his field?

She did not remember feeling either distress or joy at the thought of coming home, of living with her parents again. She was fourteen, and had skipped two grades, so she was on track to graduate at sixteen. She was considered good-looking; she wore clothes well. She had a decent bust and a narrow waist; her legs were long and slim. She gave an impression of tautness; she gave the impression that given the right opportunity she could run a mile in a minute; she could dance all night.

It was implied by the faculty wives that she was not her mother's daughter. Her mother was not one of them. Her mother put her hair up in a chignon in the morning, donned a white coat and sensible shoes, and went to her lab. Sometimes she was gone before Susan was up. A note on the kitchen table in her mother's scrawl (her neat writing she reserved for lab notes): *Bye, darling, had to run. Be back seven or so for dinner.* The cursive slanted forward, bent under her mother's urgency to return to her experiment. Something was either going well or not well. Whatever it was, the lab required her presence. Required it. Like a problem child, Susan thought. Or a king.

Susan's new friends, Laura, Antonia, and Penny, were serious girls like her. Laura's father was a banker. Antonia's parents were both lawyers, unusual for the time, but then so was having two parents who were scientists.

Penny Bogdon was the only one who seemed to come from somewhat normal circumstances. Her father was a doctor; her mother, president of the garden club. They all envied Penny with her placid, plant-obsessed mother who sat smoking Chesterfields at the kitchen table, regaling them after school with stories of boyfriends, first dates, first proms, even a first kiss—on a porch swing on a summer's evening.

Susan never asked her mother for stories, discouraged by the vague wave of dismissal her mother gave when she broached the subject, say, of love. "Oh, that—" Susan's mother said. "Why do you care?" You couldn't fight a tone like that, steel balls clacking one against the other.

The airport was on the outskirts of town. A long, grassy strip lush in the late September heat. In the open hangar, the tiny planes rested, docile insects, lovingly caged, and all facing, Susan noted, the runway field, as though to welcome the incoming and bid farewell to the outgoing. A small stable of friendly hosts. Joining them at six o'clock in the morning, she and Christopher and one old gent named Sam, who was thrilled that their tiny amateur's airport was being used to reunite a mother and father and son.

"Stood right here when my son came in from Vietnam. Alive, thank God. Whole." Sam paused. "And not so whole."

Christopher, who had held up well so far, leaned on Susan's arm, casting his gaze back toward the airplanes. "What time is it?"

A light wind blew on their cheeks. Surprisingly warm for the hour. "Early," Susan said. "Six. Peter's coming in. Peter, our son, is flying in any minute."

"What time is it?"

Susan sighed. "Six," she said. "Six, six, six."

She felt the vibration first in the soles of her feet, then she was pointing at the sky, toward the horizon of gamy clouds. Coming over the trees, the shiny nose of Peter's plane burst into sight. Peter at the controls. Peter flying! A miracle, even though Susan could easily explain the aerodynamics of flight.

Christopher gripped her arm tighter. He, too, was excited by the roar of the engine and the sight of the plane. He beamed and waved like a child at a parade. Suddenly, the plane's roar slowed to a guttural splutter of beats and breaths as it turned for the final descent.

Christopher ducked his head into the crook of his arm.

"Don't be scared, darling. It's Peter. *Our* Peter. Landing. Airplane." Susan stroked his hair, jostled his arm. "Look up now. Look!"

The plane was landing, the propellers' wind kicking up twigs, whirling up bits of leaves like confetti. The wings seemed to vibrate in her chest. Christopher, terrified, clutched her arm.

Peter was wearing, as always, his river shorts, a T-shirt, and a pair of rubber-soled sandals. Not an accidental tourist, but an imprudent one. One who forgot to change into fall clothes at the airport.

But Peter didn't look as though he were suffering. He didn't look as though he registered the temperature or even, particularly, his surroundings. He was focused instead on his parents, his arms outstretched for them both. He came forward calmly, as though there were nothing unusual in finding his father clinging like a frightened child to his mother's arm.

"Dad," he said, planting a kiss on his father's cheek. "How ya doing?"

No reply.

Peter withdrew. "Mom." He dropped his small duffel on the pavement.

"Darling," Susan said, stepping close to receive his embrace. "So happy you're here." She was *so* happy, this beautiful man, her son, was here.

Behind them, Christopher stirred, lured by the duffel like a cat to cream. He reached for the duffel, hoisted it—an ancient gesture asserting itself through the murk. "Not too bad," he said.

Peter and Susan turned from their embrace to watch. For a blazing second, he was Christopher intact, Peter's dad, her husband, who never once let his wife or son carry their own bag.

Then the duffel dropped, and Christopher burst into tears.

Later, in the car on the way home, Susan found herself glancing in the rearview mirror to catch a glimpse of Peter. A rude introduction, she thought. Christopher's confusion, his tears. But to her relief, Peter remained calm throughout. His manner suggested that nothing, really nothing, could faze him—a porters' revolt, a miscalculated food drop, a father's dementia. She wished she had that same cool. Of course, people would say she did. But all week she had been in a tailspin, wondering how to make Peter most welcome.

She had planned to cook—curried chicken; lentil stew; apple pie. For the first time in a year, she had studied a cookbook, bought the latest issue of *Gourmet* at the checkout counter. She penciled lists of ingredients. First by recipe and then by category—fruits, vegetables, meats, cheeses, desserts. She could do this, she told herself. She could do things right.

Fresh flowers in his room; guest towels; matching sheets. Crazy, she told herself, but she wanted to do things right.

Then life had intervened. She'd never actually been a good hostess. Despite their large house, she'd insisted that Christopher design a guest wing complete with small kitchen and bath. She couldn't stand being "invaded" as she put it. Even the closest of friends grated on her after a few hours.

"You hate people," Christopher once said. "Face it. That's your problem."

She bridled at this. "I love people, it's *Homo sapiens* I can't stand."

"Exactly my point."

"But it's not true. I love . . ." And Susan had ticked off a series of names—college friends, colleagues, distant relatives. "I just can't stand them in my house."

Christopher, on the other hand, loved to entertain. He was continually offering the use of their "great hall," as he called it, "the living room," Susan corrected in private, to friends, clubs, university departments to hold their parties.

"On one condition," Susan would say. "I'm allowed to disappear." But she rarely managed to do this. And so she was thought of as a hostess, a rather good one, though Susan chalked it up to a lack of bravery—she simply couldn't leave her house to strangers and go off to her lab.

But Peter was seeing the new house for the first time, and she found herself, foolishly, she knew, wanting his approval. She didn't expect him to like it, she told herself, but she did want him to feel comfortable, and to believe she had done the right thing, moving up here.

They were driving down Main Street. Susan could have taken

another route to avoid the lights, but she wanted Peter to get a sense of the town.

"What do you think?" Susan asked as they passed the row of brick storefronts, each with a striped awning, something the chamber had cooked up to appeal to tourists.

"Sort of Norman Rockwell," Peter said.

"Hopper," she said, feeling the most peculiar urge to defend her new town. "See the corner diner with all that plate glass? I think of that Hopper—whatever it's called—every time I go by."

"You come down here a lot?"

"We have our routine. Coffee at the Cup. Then we walk to the library. Very cozy."

"The right scale."

Susan smiled. "Exactly. Keeps things simple."

"And it works?"

Susan braked gently for the red light, patting the now quiet Christopher on the thigh. "So far, so good."

Christopher blinked, shifted his weight slightly forward, his fingertips resting on the dash as though it might move off without him. "Daddy home," he said.

Peter in the backseat cleared his throat. "Peter home, Dad. Peter. Me."

With her peripheral vision, Susan checked Christopher's face for a sign of recognition, a sign of anything. But there was no sign. Unless you could count the fact that Christopher relaxed his grip on the dash, closed his eyes, sank his head back against the seat, which Susan counted, she most certainly did.

It seemed to her that Peter had always had a soothing effect on his father, even as a little boy when Peter had insisted that his father teach him how to fish.

He'd already observed the hollows along the stream bank where the sunnies loafed, and all he needed, he'd said, was worms, a rod, and a hook. At first, Christopher had been patient, but then he'd grown restless, envisioning a stone bridge across the water, which he'd tried to recruit Peter to help him build. It was a favorite family story, how at last Christopher had exhausted himself moving rocks and finally settled next to Peter on the bank, how Peter, who had never fished before, instructed his father on how to *think like a fish* and *be still*. That night father and son filleted the sunnies and pan-fried them in crumbs and butter. Proudly, they'd served her the fresh-caught fish. The best meal, they agreed for years and years after, they'd ever had.

When they all got out of the car, Peter began walking down the driveway in the opposite direction of the house. He stopped about ten yards away and turned, scanning the house's façade. Susan would have appreciated help with Christopher, but she didn't say anything because Peter looked so engaged at that moment, like a hunting dog filtering the air for a scent, its nose conducting a private symphony of curiosity and desire. Then Peter moved back up the driveway.

"Roof's in good shape, but you've got hornets." He pointed first to a papery cone bulging above the front door light, then to a wartlike lump beside a second-floor window. "I'll knock them down before I go."

They entered the house through the side door into the kitchen, and while Susan helped Christopher out of his coat, Peter went into the living room.

"Wow. When did you get this?"

She gathered from Peter's tone that he'd discovered Christopher's La-Z-Boy. It was the sort of thing that might shock him.

"That's Dad's chair. He finds it soothing." On cue, Christopher ambled to the smooth, satiny boat of a chair and slid in.

"TV, too?"

A big black television sat installed like a fat Buddha in a cabinet across from Christopher's blue chair, a television several times larger than any they'd owned before.

"He can't watch anymore. The voices confuse him. I use it for videos. My yoga tapes."

"You do yoga?" Peter had perched himself on the arm of Christopher's chair and was lightly massaging his father's upper back. Christopher's eyes were closed.

"A little. Do you?"

Peter shook his head.

"You don't need it. You're limber."

Peter smoothed his palms over the tops of his thighs. "So where are you putting me?"

"Oh, your room. Second door, left. Next to ours. It's a mess, I'm afraid. Didn't have time to make up the bed or even clear a path between the boxes."

She followed him up the stairs, standing in the shadow of the hall while she watched him flick on the light. "Oh," she said. "Worse than I thought. I'm sorry."

Peter dropped his duffel on the threshold and started to stack boxes. "Where I'm trekking it can take an hour to move a foot."

"Quicksand?"

"Marancae grass."

"Your thesis!" she said.

"Come to haunt me."

"Oh well, then. Boxes are nothing."

"Do you miss people?" Susan asked. She and Peter were in the kitchen washing up dishes, putting things away. She had already put Christopher to bed. Not so difficult given his medications.

Peter had spent most of the day on the telephone and on his computer. There were still so many details to work out for the

"Mega-Trek," as he called it. Susan had tried not to be disappointed, but this was impossible. He was here and not here. So much like her parents, like Christopher now.

Peter looked at her. "I was going to ask you the same thing."

"Me?" Susan swiped the back of a soapy hand across her cheekbone, leaving more soap. "Do I seem isolated?"

"Quite."

"Your father's enough company for me. Molly Tyne, Fred Hamblin, the people at work—totally draining at this point."

Peter nodded as he wiped a wineglass with a cloth towel his mother had handed him. "I suppose I'm the same, really. I can't stand to be anywhere near civilization."

"Don't you take it with you?"

He looked at her sharply, still Susan plunged on. "I mean you have your Pygmies, the conservation people, reporters—"

"They only stay a week or so. I'm not allowing any hangers-on for this expedition. I want to do this pretty much alone."

Susan laughed. "You've always felt that way. Ever since you were little, six or so, hiking in the Adirondacks, you had to lead, had to be on your own up front, you'd start running when Dad and I caught up to you."

"Brat."

Susan shook her head. "Believe me, I understood. I'm the same way." But what she wanted to know, did he get lonely as she now did? Did he ever just need someone?

Peter set the second wineglass in the cupboard, turned to face Susan. The cleanup was done and suddenly Susan felt awkward. The worry of a date turning sour, the shyness of ardor. Was any of hers for Peter requited?

Peter rested his slim hips against the counter, crossed his arms. "So what's really going on here?"

"What's it look like?"

"Dad seems worse. Tons worse since I saw him last year."

Susan shrugged. "Going to hell in a handbasket, I guess."

"Tell me."

Should she? She had vowed not to be one of those mothers whose needs stood in the way. "It's horrible. He's gone. I'm not equipped." She held her hands up in the air, but her face was falling, eyelids, cheeks, jowls. She shook her head hard against the grief. She hadn't meant to reveal all of this. She wasn't one of those mothers to impose a burden on her child. She had promised herself she wasn't going to fall apart. But here she was. "Bed," she said at last. By avoiding his eyes, she could cross the kitchen without cracking. "Exhaustion." She gave a feeble wave.

"Mom," Peter said. His tone was serious, concerned.

She halted, but did not look at him. It felt silly, but she simply could not look.

"How about I take him somewhere tomorrow?"

"Somewhere?" For a wild instant, Susan thought Peter meant an institution, a nursing home. It came as a relief.

"For a drive. You can get a break."

She nodded, holding her left hand at her temple like a blinder or a shield. "Fine. Great. Good. Thank you." That was all she could manage as she headed to the stairs.

The morning after Peter's arrival, Susan rose early. Her plan was to enjoy a half hour of silence in which to sip her coffee and think her thoughts. Beside her on the bed, Christopher was still a sleeping lump beneath the covers, a snoring mountain. Thank God he slept so deeply and so well, she thought as she crept lightly out the door and across the hall to the bathroom. She'd always arisen earlier than Christopher and it was these early mornings that saved her now. For long minutes she could sustain the illusion that their life was what it had always been.

This morning Susan decided to skip her shower; Peter liked to get up early, too. A race of the early birds, the prize—the sort of King of the Hill glory of being the only one up.

The light streaming in through the kitchen windows already contained a hint of the color it would ripen to during the course of the late September day.

Peter looked up from his laptop. "Morning. Hope I didn't wake you."

Trying not to betray the slightest surprise or irritation, Susan shook her head. "How're things in Gabon?"

"Shitty. Porters are threatening to strike—"

"You haven't even started—"

Ignoring her, Peter started typing quickly, rattling the computer keys with more pique than she remembered him possessing. But whether it was directed toward her or the wily porters she couldn't tell. "Sorry. I'm in real time. Don't want them to sign off on the other end—" Peter scanned the new message on the screen then began stabbing again at the keys. "I don't *have* a hell of a lot of money!"

Susan was aware that Peter was talking to himself—or to his correspondent—not to her. She stood still, listening, fascinated.

"*Not* the issue. They're scared. We've got to deal with *that*."

"Why are they scared?" Susan asked. From behind Peter's shoulder, she could see tiny navy letters flash on the pale white screen.

"For most of these guys, it's like getting on a boat that's sailing around the world when you're convinced the world is flat. They think they're going to die."

"Very scary. How do you get around that?"

"Money. Decent food. A good leader."

"Kemo sabe."

Peter flushed and cut his eyes away from the screen to glare at her. "My point man, Mouko. He's a Congolese Pygmy. Sixty years old, fucking brilliant—and strong. No one wields a machete better than Mouko, or has better endurance. He keeps me going. Couldn't do it without him."

"What do you pay him?"

Peter, frowning, pushed a button and closed the screen. "What's gotten into you?"

Susan shook her head. "Do you see your whole life like this, then? Planning expeditions, raising funds, living mainly over there?" Never coming home.

"I *have* been doing this most of my life, Mother."

"And so it will continue?"

"Unless I'm skewered by a rogue elephant. Or sidelined by an angry potentate."

"Or can't find funding."

"Good-bye, bad fairy." He waved her away, turning back to his computer. "I've got a couple more e-mails to send."

"Any coffee left?"

"No, made it all for me. *Joke*, Mother. Would you like me to pour you some?"

She shook her head, ashamed of herself. What more could she want *for her son*—this handsome man with the corded legs and arms tanned the color of cinnamon—than for him to be happy? He was. She could tell. He was so at ease talking about his life over there, his plans. So confident of himself in that world. Was she jealous of Mouko? Or that Peter had a Mouko in his life—an indefatigable partner, a helpmeet? Someone she had once had in Christopher, now lost for good? She tsked in disgust at herself. The thought of her own irritability exhausted her.

She poured her coffee. Then tipped in milk from a small

ceramic pitcher Peter had been thoughtful enough to fill. Indeed, the gentian blue mug (her favorite), the spoon, the milk had all been set out on the counter, waiting for her. Through the window above the sink, she could see that it was a beautiful fall morning. A perfect day, the sky clearing in the east to blue; some leaves already bewitched with fire. Maybe she ought to tell him, maybe she ought to tell Peter now what she truly felt. Maybe she ought to tell him that she missed him, missed him desperately, that his leaving again felt like a rope tossed to a drowning woman, a rope tossed from a boat, speeding away, leaving no chance to grasp its ragged end.

She turned to face him and saw that he was now fingering the buttons in the bowl on the table. "Your dad's," she began to explain. "They soothe him."

Peter stopped groping. He pushed the bowl away. "If I could help, I would."

He would, but he can't, and she will not demand it. "I manage better on my own."

"Says who?"

Susan felt the nodes in her armpits begin to prick. She would have liked to incinerate Peter just then for what he didn't know. But she refrained. "Let's discuss the plan for today. I thought we might give Dad a bath this morning. That is something I could use help with." She wouldn't tell Peter about the times Christopher had raised a fist or the day he wielded the plunger like a mallet when she suggested he step in the shower.

"Mom." Peter stood up and went to her. Clearly he wanted to hold her, comfort her, but Susan gripped her mug to her chest like a shield, averted her gaze.

"Mom, I just wanted—"

"Don't tell me what to do. Don't, don't."

"No one's telling you—"

"You are. You drop in here for a day or two and think you can tell me. You don't know what it takes to have to explain to someone. To educate someone who doesn't know Christopher. The real Christopher. That kind of understanding is essential—"

"Crap," Peter said, backing off, turning away. He scooped his computer from the table, then faced her from where he stood. "You know, Mom, you really haven't changed. So *fucking* stubborn. 'Kiss me, I'm a stoic.'"

Susan couldn't resist a smile. "I see it more as hubris. 'Pride goeth before destruction, and a haughty spirit before a fall.'"

Peter snorted lightly. "That, too."

But really, Susan thought, *why can't anyone give me credit? Why can't anyone call me Antigone: loyal, devoted caretaker of the doomed and the denigrated?*

The moan from above sounded like a dog's lost cry, like the springer spaniel who lived next door to their old house and cried until his owners returned. Christopher's moaning could drive you crazy, too, unless you thought of it as wind through winter trees.

"I'll get him," Susan said, heading for the stairs.

Peter followed.

From the bedroom door they could both see the covers twitching, undulating over Christopher's flailing attempts to get out from under them.

In a second, Susan had set Christopher free, unveiled him. He sat upright, his legs sprawled in front of him, his shirt opened and twisted so that an arm hung exposed above the row of buttons. He looked like a drunk after a bad night, a sort of cartoon.

"Dad," Peter said. He moved toward his father so swiftly that Christopher flinched as though he expected to be hit.

"Slow down," Susan commanded. "He doesn't know you." She came around the end of the bed, wedging her hip next to Christopher's.

Peter stopped. His arms slack at his sides. "I can't believe this," he said. "I just can't."

Susan ignored him, rubbing Christopher's back, murmuring quietly to him, but the moaning continued.

"Is he in pain?" Peter asked.

Susan shook her head. She was rocking now, slowly, side to side. She could feel Christopher's ribs begin to soften against hers; his shoulders, then his torso, swaying with hers. After all these years, his smallness still surprised her, and she thought of that afternoon before their wedding day when they stood in front of the mirror at the dry cleaners and gazed at themselves in shock. *Freaks*, they gasped, and laughed.

"Easy, easy," Susan soothed. Her fingertips traced a circle on Christopher's back, and his moaning kept on coming, rising and releasing in trembling waves, a keening that seemed to contain all the sadness of the world.

Then switching her tone and pointing her chin to Peter, Susan said in an urgent whisper, "Get the bath going. Not too hot." And seeing Peter still frozen there, a man in shock, she summoned a sterner tone. "Now."

Then came the part of the visit she could look back on with something approaching awe. How smoothly the bath had gone. How amazing Peter's skills were. He handled his father so gently. Gentleness was a trait she knew in him through the way he'd cared for the creatures he brought home from the woods, broken creatures: crows and robins with damaged wings; abandoned bunnies; baby squirrels. He tended them in the shed behind the house and released them when they had healed. She didn't interfere. The shed was Peter's lab, so to speak. The animals, his projects.

Now he eased his naked father into the bath; massaging his bony foot; introducing him to the water as though his father were blind. "The water is your friend, Dad. Good water." And his father ventured a big toe, then a whole foot into the shallow bath. Quickly Peter stripped to his shorts and stepped in with him. How brilliant, Susan thought. She'd never thought of bathing with Christopher! Supporting his father's back with one hand, Peter sat on the edge of the tub, his feet in the water, and began to soap the old man's legs. Christopher looked down at his own knees in surprise. "Nice," he said.

"Knees," Peter replied. "Nice knees."

Christopher smiled.

Then Peter handed him the washcloth and his father took it, dabbing at his penis gingerly. "Nice," he said. "Nice nice."

Peter stood up and took the cloth again and dipped it into the water and soaped Christopher's back. He told stories of watching hippos bathe—the wonder that anything so earthbound could float.

"Hip-po," Christopher said. "Hip-po, hip-po, hip-po."

"Hippo," Peter echoed and Christopher smiled and looked to Susan who spiked the first syllable then drove the second down.

"HIP-po," she affirmed. She wanted to leap up, to shout for joy, to stomp out a whooping dance of exultation. But she kept herself quiet, mouthing a silent *Go Peter!* as she handed him a towel.

Still standing in the tub, Peter wrapped the towel around Christopher's shoulders and patted him the way he had been toweled by her when he was a little boy. When they stepped out, Susan was ready with Christopher's big shirt; his shorts; his fleece pants.

"Thank you, honey," she said. "Thank you, thank you." She

reached a kiss up to his cheek. He squeezed her shoulder in reply.

Christopher, clean and bathed, smelled like almonds.

The morning was still beautiful; sun bright; temperature holding at 68 degrees when Peter, good to his word, bundled his father into the car. She had two hours for certain. Three, if Christopher fell asleep in the car.

Three hours. Don't be greedy. Two or three hours of freedom. Susan sat at the kitchen table after they left and spun in a vortex of desires: read? write? catch up on mail? sleep? stretch? walk? eat? She wanted to do everything and nothing. To be in public and to stay in private. To publish a scientific paper and polish off a detective novel. To pay bills and to spend money.

To clean. This last surprised her. House cleaning had always been the least of her priorities (and besides, she used to hire someone to do it). But now she looked around and noticed the sticky patches on the linoleum floor. The scribbled nests of white hairs, her own, beneath the chair legs. She sighed, thinking suddenly of the rest of the house—the stained toilet, the crumb-filled carpets. The only upkeep she managed was the dishes and the laundry. Long ago Molly Tyne had dubbed dishwashing "hydrotherapy." After her divorce, Molly washed every dish and pot in the house and came over to Susan's to do the same. "It's great," Molly said. "You turn your back on the world and soap."

She preferred laundry, she told Molly. Measuring, sorting, then, with the spin of a purring dial, letting the machine take over.

Molly laughed. "That's the scientist," she said. She didn't bother to explain.

Susan got up from the table. She had an electric broom somewhere; a mop and a pail. The thought of locating these items made her gelatinous with fatigue. She took a couple of steps across the kitchen and it came to her—sleep. That's what she needed the most: hours of deep, deep sleep.

Peter and Christopher returned. It went swimmingly, Peter said in a faked British accent. He was game for more. And Christopher, though mute, seemed calm.

And so the next two days, Peter drove Christopher around the countryside—and Susan slept.

Each day she felt better and better. The miraculous feeling that she was returning to her own true self.

"You see, you're reviving," Peter said. "Check out home help."

Perhaps it was time. Look how quickly and quietly Christopher had accepted Peter even though he didn't seem to know who Peter was.

Or did he? Christopher rarely spoke in her and Peter's presence. Occasionally he erupted as though in mid-thought. Something about a "man-nee." Or was it a "man-a-tee"? Susan thought of those large placid mammals as kin to Christopher. Could he be making a connection? A joke even?

Peter disagreed. "It's someone he wants to see. Someone he needs to reconnect with. That first day he kept repeating the same thing—'the man-nee over caf-fee.' Something like that. 'The man at the café,' I think he's saying. Is there someone he particularly likes to visit there?"

Susan shook her head. "It's not pidgin. 'The man-nee' could be anyone or anything—or nothing. Bubbles breaking the surface."

"I don't believe that," Peter said. They were sitting at the kitchen table after lunch. Christopher still wore a plastic bib clipped to his collar. Peter sat beside him, spooning pureed organic carrot into his father's mouth and mincing his father's spaghetti (he had a tendency to choke).

And while Susan felt grateful and light—her first unencumbered meal in months—she was aware of a stab of jealousy as well. Why was Christopher so agreeable with Peter? It was as though he'd chosen the favorite parent for whom he would behave.

Peter took up his father's hand, stroking his fingers. "Man-nee, Daddy. Who the 'man-nee'?"

Christopher stared at Peter and then glanced at his hand in Peter's hand and withdrew it.

"See? It isn't simple."

"I think I knew that," Peter said. He leaned his elbows on the table so that his face was level with hers. "I really do understand—"

"You can't."

Peter turned his face from hers and sat back in his chair as he tapped the closed lid of his laptop. That computer reminded Susan of a faithful dog, always near at hand, always at the ready. She'd begun to hate it.

"You've got to make that call. Get someone in here. I wish I could help—"

"I know."

"Find someone."

Susan glanced at Christopher, who pawed his buttons, absorbed. "Can't." She was afraid if her lips parted further, she'd break down.

"Why not?"

She shook her head in tiny, almost imperceptible arcs. *He needs me.*

"Well, I just found out that the porters are on board, and I've got to get to Gabon pronto or the deal's going to fall apart. I have to leave, Mom."

"Tomorrow?"

Peter nodded.

Susan drew her thumb and middle finger down the sides of her face, eye socket to jawline, finger on bone. The velvet layer of skin beneath her touch somehow reassuring. "I'm going to miss you."

"A day program, Mom. There have got to be some day programs in the area. I know there's at least one. I looked it up yesterday." Peter fished in his pocket for a scrap of paper, which he pushed across the table. "I drove past. An old Victorian. Big porch. Not far from here."

Susan stared at the paper, but did not pick it up. "I've seen it."

"Take him. Now."

"You can't just barge in."

"You can't?"

"Getting him in, getting him out. A strange place. You have no idea."

"Last chance, Mom. Come on. While I'm still here."

Susan swept the paper into her palm. Peter had never gone to day care. She just couldn't trust anyone else to do it right. Instead she brought Peter to work. Her colleagues thought her a lunatic and tried to have her banned from faculty meetings. They couldn't. Seated in a wingback chair in a corner of the faculty room, a paisley shawl draped over Peter at her breast, she was prepared to lecture anyone who challenged her on the scientifically proven benefits of breast-feeding, from the study of primates to the theories of attachment to the effect of nucleic acids on the immune system.

But at times thoughts came to her too horrible to be spoken aloud or even committed to paper: *What if I'd been on my own? What if I hadn't had any distractions at all? What would I have discovered?*

"All right," she said. "I'll call. We'll take a look. But we might not leave the car."

The drive was short; Christopher, though confused, was not agitated.

Peter got out first. Susan, with Christopher, took her time. She hoped the giddiness she was feeling did not translate to Christopher. Carefully, she wrapped his arm around hers, lifted her chin, and took a deep breath. They might appear to be retirees on an afternoon stroll, or a sister with her older brother.

The house, a cheery salmon pink, was wrapped with a wide front porch on which sat a row of elderly men and women in rocking chairs. One man raised his hand, a greeting or a warning, Susan couldn't tell. The house with its generous front porch, its large windows, reminded her of some place, some house she'd visited before. A childhood home? A friend's home? Her mind flinched. David Kappelman's house.

Halfway up the slate walk, Christopher stopped short and planted his feet hips' width apart, his lips parted slightly, and his face took on an expression of uncertainty mixed with awe, as though he were a little boy contemplating the ocean.

Wait, Susan wanted to call out to Peter, who was already on the front porch, already ringing the bell, but her attention was diverted by Christopher's tug on her arm. Had he read her mind? Or had she read his? Or were they of one mind, united as they had once been? Clearly, he was trying to turn her back in the direction they'd come.

Ahead, Susan could see that someone had opened the front door. Someone was questioning Peter. Susan could hear the pitch of a young woman's voice as she wheeled to keep abreast of Christopher. It didn't matter. She would explain.

High above, a seam burst in the clouds, releasing a sudden spotlight of shimmering gold that seemed to follow them as they strode, arm in arm, back to the car.

TWENTY-FOUR

A YELLOW HELICOPTER HAD BEEN DRONING ALL MORNING since they got back from the diner, circling above the farm and the woods. His grandfather, who did not like to notice anything, noticed this. He stood in the freezing barnyard and looked up at the sky, resenting trouble. Then he shifted his gaze to the boy standing a little distance off where the ground was chewed, churned in the last thaw by the hooves of pigs.

Corey said nothing. His mind was circling like the helicopter: *Should I tell? Should I tell?* He could see the man asleep in the snow, still dreaming of running, but running nowhere. His grand-father was right. He wanted to be a hero, The Boy Who Found the Man, but he wasn't sure he'd be seen that way. He might be the boy who found the dead man. The stone-cold dead man. It could be his fault. Like it was before.

Corey and his grandfather were cleaning manure out of the gutters in the barn when the conveyer belt jammed. "Shit," said his grandfather. "Go get me a wrench."

The tools were in the shop off the tractor shed, kitty corner to the barn. Opening the door of the shed, Corey smelled kero-sene, a smell that made him think of clean-shaven men and sharp blades and fire. A smell that reached through his body and shook his gut. A kind of ecstasy.

You're after the wrench, he told himself.

The wrenches hung like thighbones along the shop wall. He looked at them, wondering which one his grandfather meant, hoping he could figure it out somehow. But he didn't know exactly what his grandfather wanted it for. His gaze slid to the littlest one, barely used, still shiny, and then up to the largest one, grown brown with rust.

On the shelf below the wrenches rested the lantern his grandfather used when the electricity went out in the barn, and beside it, the large square can of kerosene with which to fill it. Next to that, a box of wooden matches, the cardboard top sagging and soft. Kerosene and matches. The way Lance would see it, a kind of invitation.

Get the wrench. He reached for one in the middle and ran back with it to the barn.

In the barn, his grandfather was crouched up by the wheel of the conveyer where it angled to an opening above the manure heap. "Bring it here," he said.

Corey stepped onto the black, sludgy tongue of the gutter, careful to fit the heel of his boot to the lip on the conveyer to keep from slipping back. His grandfather was working bare-handed, even though he had gloves. He didn't care about getting cow shit on him, but Corey did. He couldn't get used to the smell, or the way it looked on the ground, puddles of horrible dark pudding.

Without looking up, his grandfather reached out for the wrench, hooked it over the center bolt, and twisted hard. Down below, the cows were working their cuds, pissing streams of yellow pee, breathing clouds that looked like smoke. Cows didn't care about nothing but themselves, Corey thought. They didn't have to.

"Oughta do it," his grandfather grunted. He handed back the wrench.

That was his cue. He hopped off the gutter and picked up the black plug. His job was to stick it into the socket. But first he waited for his grandfather to get down. If he didn't do that, his grandfather'd go for a ride round the end of the conveyer and off the end into the pile. You could suffocate in there if someone didn't pull you out.

His grandfather stepped off the gutter onto the concrete floor, wiping his dirty hands on the thighs of his overalls. Corey stuck the round black plug in the socket and the belt chugged to life.

"Sonofabitch," his grandfather said, "we did it," and for a second, Corey felt proud. He tried hard to do everything right.

Before lunch, Corey washed his hands and face at the kitchen sink. His grandmother was particular about that, especially hands. There couldn't be any dirt under the nails or in the cracks of the knuckles, or any smell at all of the cow barn on your palms. If there was, you had to go back to wash them all over again.

Above the sink was a small window, crawling with flies. No matter how cold or dark, there were always flies. As he dried his hands on the cloth towel, thoughts were working in him, worries that plagued him much worse than whether there was dirt on his hands. *Should he tell before the helicopter found the man? Should he tell he didn't do nothing? If he did, would they believe him?*

His grandmother was at the stove. On Saturdays and Sundays, lunch was like dinner, the biggest meal. His grandfather was already sitting down. Boots changed for slippers over woolen socks. Clean flannel shirt and clean farmer pants. He had his bad leg out and his paper up, reading what he hadn't finished in the morning.

Lunch was hash. Small pieces of reddish pork and potatoes and bits of pepper all stirred together in an iron skillet. His grandmother served them. First his grandfather, then him, then herself. Then she set the skillet on a potholder in the middle of the table and said grace to herself. She didn't even look at his hands.

Should he tell?

He didn't know much about his grandmother. She was his father's mother, but she didn't talk about that and she didn't show pictures. No one in his family did.

Today, after grace, she sat with her fork at the edge of her plate, like she was waiting for something, waiting for his grandfather. *Maybe they knew.* Usually his grandfather was hungry and the paper snapped shut as soon as the plate arrived. Not today. Today the sides of the paper came together like slow wings and he folded once, twice, and picked up his fork and did not look at the boy's grandmother.

His grandmother sat, chin forward and lips pursed. She did not move.

Usually if his grandfather was eating, they all were. But should he eat or not? His grandfather wasn't eating. He was stirring the hash with the tips of his fork, stirring it like a little kid, looking for the plate.

What was his grandfather waiting for?

"Did you tell him?" his grandmother said at last. "Did you?"

His grandfather kept stirring and did not look up.

"You got to tell him," she said. "You're the one."

Right then he knew he couldn't eat. He put down his fork and bowed his head. The *he* had to be him. They had to know.

"All right," his grandfather said. He set his fork on end so the tines curved toward the boy like an upside-down pitchfork. "You're leaving," he said. "We can't keep you no more."

Twenty-five

"Did I miss anything?"

Jeff looks up from the map on the coffee table at Susan, who pauses on her way downstairs to smooth a wisp of mussed hair around her ear. It is around noon, a few hours since they last spoke, but he can tell instantly that she is herself again: practical, composed. Though who could blame her for being upset this morning with the helicopter waking her, the dogs, the cold. Anyone in her position would be losing it by now, and most would not find themselves quite so alone. "It's snowing lightly. We're pushing into a new quadrant, but no news."

She crosses the room, tucking herself neatly onto the sofa across from him. "Snowing. Is that a good thing?"

"Can be." *If the object of the search can still make tracks.* To his relief, she moves on as though her thoughts hit a bumper at the same time as his and veered off.

"Have you ever been lost?"

"Have I lost someone?" Good to keep her talking off topic, Jeff thinks. It's the tangents that will keep you sane.

"Been lost. You. As a child. I suppose everyone's had that experience." She reaches for the glass of water she left on the coffee table. She drinks. "For some reason that's on my mind."

Lost. No. Not as a kid, but as a man, a young man. Clips of the jungle flash through his mind. Night gear. Point man. "I was in 'Nam."

"Oh," she says. "My friends were lucky. We were a bit too privileged."

He nods. He likes her honesty.

"I had a dream just now. Horrible dream. I'd lost Peter, my son. Left him somewhere. Dropped him off, alone, at a drugstore. I was running late—I'm always late—always relying on another mother to pick him up, take him home. So I guess it was the other mother who dropped him off. I called the school. No answer. And finally I reach the secretary. She's screaming at me, 'You left the child alone, alone by himself . . .' Can you believe it? I'm still shaking. I'm still feeling as though I'd left him somewhere. I'm still feeling guilty."

"Have *you* ever been lost, Susan?"

"Come to think of it, my parents left *me* once."

"Left you?"

"Yes. In a pharmacy. In Pasadena. It was incredibly hot, I remember. And humid. So humid you could barely walk. My parents were at a conference at Cal Tech—"

"What's that?"

Susan squints at him. "Oh, sorry. California Institute of Technology. The MIT of the—well, the best science university in the West."

Jeff nods. "I was only in California once. Shipping back."

Susan stares down at her fingers, spreading them, then flexing them into fists. "Why am I going on like this?"

"It's all right. No one's losing focus. I've been in touch with Higgs and the others. It's going along. Everyone's doing their best." He can feel her mind alight on this and finds himself willing her not to dwell. He doesn't want to tell her that some of the firefighters are still stomping around in full fucking gear, that the volunteers have trampled any possible remaining tracks, that Christopher is probably dead.

"It's amazing to me how well I remember that pharmacy. A ceiling fan with wide wooden blades and black and white tile on the floor. Like a mixed-up crossword. The store was on a corner, a triangular building, the door at its apex. I thought this was wonderful.

"I remember the entrance was almost blocked by metal carrels filled with comic books, which my parents didn't allow me to read, so I grabbed a bunch, feeling as though I'd stolen someone's flowers, and sat down at the lunch counter—

"I'd brought my own books, *Anne of Green Gables*, *The Prince and the Pauper*, but instead of unloading my bag, I spied on myself in the mirror behind the counter, wondering who that was with the stack of *Archies* and a strawberry soda. I was working on this problem of objectifying myself, trying to see if I could become a total stranger to the girl in the glass."

"Did it work?"

"Haven't you had that experience? Staring at yourself so long you become an imposter?"

He shakes his head, but suddenly he is seeing himself this morning, staring at his face in the mirror above the bathroom sink. An old mirror, freckled where the silver had flaked off. Even through the mirror's blotches, he'd gotten the idea. His face was wide, his cheekbones reddened. His eyes were what women liked. They were blue and green, fissured. They changed with the light. Almost every woman he'd ever talked to mentioned his eyes up front. Except Leanne. And Susan.

You're a woman, Leanne'd said to him the first time she looked hard in his eyes. Not in anger. In wonder. She thought of herself as the man. The one with force. She'd taken him so fiercely on that night and so many nights after. Rolling him on his back, stripping him down, thrusting herself against him, bone to bone.

But she left him for a boy.

"How old were you, Susan?"

"Ten. Eleven. I thought of myself as very grown-up."

He can picture her, a slim, straight girl with serious eyes. "Your parents just left you there?"

"It was out of the heat; there was someone to look out for me (though it took the soda jerk a while to figure that out); I wasn't going to *starve*."

"How long?"

"Hours, I think. I ran out of comic books and had to go back to the real books. I don't remember being angry about it. It was the way children were treated in those days."

Jeff raises his eyebrows. "These days you'd find yourself under my jurisdiction."

Susan smiles. "Really? Are you a judge of some sort?"

"Caseworker. Juveniles. Juvenile fire starters. I do a lot of fire education." Ah, how Leanne would scoff at the last. Mr. Rescuer can't think of no one but himself, he can hear her say. Not true. He's always thinking of others. That's the problem. He's always thinking of the kids no one wants to think of—the kids who burn down their house, barns, sheds. Murder their kith and kin, and don't even know that they're crying for help. His help.

"That sounds extremely difficult."

"It is."

"So what can you do? They must come from abuse or mental illness."

"The youngest fire starters, the ones who might be innocent, get to watch a PowerPoint on my laptop. They click the keys while Mr. Herdman tells them a story: this is the inside of a house. Click. This is a house that's just been burned. Click. This is a house where somebody died. Click." The light from the screen bleaches their pale faces, while he watches for some sign of understanding, of remorse—even fear. Can they connect the images to their actions? Can they connect at all? They turn their faces to him, eager and alight. The computer's cool. Can they keep it? Please, Mr. Herdman. Please?

"Do they know what they've done?"

"Most don't remember, or if they do, it's a blur." Which reminds him. Byer. Poor damn kid. Each time the judge's gavel hit, the boy jerked in his seat like he was catching it between his shoulder blades. He caught it all right. Jeff sighs, not wanting to think about it. Something about that kid, he wanted to jump up and yell, "He's innocent!" He didn't, though. No one would have believed him.

Susan drains her water glass and sets it on the floor as she cranes toward the map. "You know if you pay too much attention to the boundaries, you're going to have trouble seeing the big picture."

"That's true," Jeff says. "Are you seeing something about the big picture?"

Susan shakes her head. "I wish I were." She picks up a legal pad with her notes written in tiny, precise waves.

He's surprised at the sparseness of evidence of what the Hunsingers' lives were before this event. In the bedroom upstairs, an open package of adult diapers; a closet heaped with clothes. In the bathroom, a medicine chest filled with vials. Someone ill lives here, not necessarily someone demented.

Outside, the crews are coming in, going out. He can hear the sounds of the engines sputtering and revving, cutting off; the radios hawking squibs of information. And in the distance the more ominous chatter of helicopter blades. It's a muted circus;

a group assembling or disassembling—it's hard to tell. But it's where he'd like to be and would be if it weren't for his goddamn gut and twinging knees.

Jeff stands up, looking now at the hangings on the wall above the empty fireplace. A mask and a statue of a naked woman carved out of ebony.

"My son sent us those," she says, positioning herself beside him.

"Oh," he says, "different."

"They're from Gabon."

"How long's it been since you've seen him?"

She frowns. "Almost five months. Yes, five months. Peter stopped here before he took off. That was September."

"You must miss him." Does her son miss her? He does not miss his own mother whom he has not actually laid eyes on for fifteen years. After his father left, his mother shed her old life: farmer's wife; churchwoman; historical society member. The new woman liked men, a lot of them; liked eye makeup and working the late shift at the truck stop. She didn't come to the party after he and Leanne got married, though he did invite her. She lives in Florida or else somewhere in Maine. Maybe even both, depending on the season. Occasionally, he gets cards, pictures of brown-stained barbecue joints or diners sprouting neon signs big as trees. Freebies. (At least she bought a stamp.) The cards are all about the weather—never too good—or her health, same, but he suspects she writes them after she or her man has moved on.

To Jeff's surprise, Susan has closed her eyes, her head shaking against whatever it is she is thinking. "Susan?"

"I said something so stupid when he was here."

"Like what?" But her head keeps wagging. She won't look at him. "Listen, Susan, at times like this all kinds of shit comes up. You can't really fight it."

She nods, pulls in her lips, and he wonders if this is it, the tsunami that almost never fails to break in these situations, triggered usually by the smallest of disturbances—a dropped glass, a broken nail, a car that won't start. His father finding his best cow down, taking the rifle, taking the checkbook, and then gone. Forever.

"Just before Peter came to visit, I happened to read a friend's paper that posited that the conservationists—Peter's group—and the logging companies were in cahoots to take over the forests, that *both* groups were colonizers."

"You mentioned this to Peter?"

"I wasn't saying I *agreed*. It wasn't meant as an attack. I just wanted him to consider the bigger picture."

"When did you say all this?"

Susan gives a sheepish look. "He was literally stepping out the door."

Why? Why would you say that? Jeff thinks.

"How come you can hear yourself saying the wrong thing, but you still can't stop?" She raises her hands, helplessly.

Or know you're doing the wrong thing, Jeff thinks. And there is Leanne again, belly as big as Santa's, telling him not to go.

TWENTY-SIX

IN THE RESCUE BUSINESS THERE IS RESCUE AND THERE IS recovery, which is ironic, Jeff thinks, because it's the recovery no one ever really recovers from. When he gets the call on his beeper, gets the code, gets the coordinates, he assures Susan that he's just going out to the tent, that he needs the air, needs to debrief.

"I'm not an idiot, Jeff," she says. "Please remember that."

In the warming tent on the front lawn, Higgs has gathered the men around the topo map, laying transparency over transparency like layers of dragonfly wings as he begins the debriefing.

The K-9 unit found the body. That is, Charlie, the German shepherd, now licking his balls under the refreshment table, and his handler, Bill. A simple belt headed them in the right direction; the belt from Christopher's raincoat; something the humans missed. Jeff joins in the clapping as he makes his way down the frozen aisle. *All in a day's work for Charlie,* Jeff thinks. *Oh, to be a dog.*

Higgs waves him closer. "How's Mrs. Hunsinger?"

"Resting."

"She knows it's a recovery?"

"She's not an idiot," Jeff says, echoing Susan.

"Well, I've just been telling everybody here more bad news. We're calling Reddin."

Jeff raises his eyebrows, while the other men stir, whispering among themselves.

"We got a burned body."

Jeff blinks hard. "You're shittin' me."

"I wish."

From his tone, Jeff believes him. "Christ. Lightning?"

"Kerosene."

"You're shitting."

"Empty gallon and matches all over the fucking place."

"Shit."

Higgs's mouth works like he's trying to keep something down. "We need Reddin."

"Suicide or homicide?" He can't see it; either one, he can't see it.

"What's it sound like to you?"

Impossible.

Already Higgs is moving off into the stirred-up hive of men around the tent. Radios crackle, an ambulance siren pinwheels down the road. And every car engine seems to start up at the same time, throwing up smoky clouds of exhaust.

Jeff strides to catch up with Higgs. "Where they headed?"

"Map 2. Clearing off G3. Gotta bag and tag."

Jeff squints, seeing a map in his mind's eye. *The woods. Deep woods.* "You want me to tell Dr. Hunsinger?" He knows the answer, he just has to hear it.

"You're the one."

Clearing the flaps of the tent, Jeff barrels into the cold air that shears his cheeks like a straight razor. Oh God. Nimble Christopher defied all wisdom, theirs and his, turned from open meadow and open road into the woods. Why? Why work so hard to get lost?

Picking his way through fallen branches, throwing a leg astride a slanting trunk, jigging it free. Continuing. Why? Why would a half-frozen old man drag himself and a can of kerosene through streams and tangled limbs to the middle of the forest, light himself on fire?

But he's seen it before. He was in the square, a leave day, a leave-it-behind-to-drink-and-screw day. He had a girl waiting for him in a room at the so-called *ho*-tel, a dark flower of a girl with cool fingers and a wet tongue. He was hurrying, late, already wrung with desperation for that refuge, that drowning place.

In the square, a crowd was forming, white-saried nuns with shaved heads, scrawny overdraped monks. Instinctively, he ducked, blinkered his eyes with his cupped hands, as he wove his way through the easily parted fringes of the crowd. A block to go. No, two. Then a cool drink. A smoke.

The shriek froze him. So loud and close, it seemed for a moment as though it had come from his own lungs or that someone had been murdered in his wake. He spun and saw what it seemed impossible to see: in the center of the square, two human forms, seated in the same postures as the Buddhas he'd seen in some of their temples—life-size and enviably still; oh to be stone, not flesh—but here was flesh mimicking stone, no, wood, the human seated forms, engulfed in flames, rippling auroras of melting air encircling the skulls that were shrinking and shriveling before his eyes. All around him, the witnesses were a screaming wall of white. He was sick then and he is sick now, remembering, seeing, not comprehending anything.

Suicide. It's the only answer after what Susan's told him. But still, impossible—the effort, the coordination, the will? How had the old man found the strength for all that?

The minute Jeff leaves, she closes the curtains, runs upstairs to lower the blinds. It's not what she intended, it's not something she planned to do. But all of a sudden, she needs the dark; she needs, for the first time in her life, not to know. Forget her urgency to crack the nut, now she'd like to seal it all up, seal herself inside its dark shell. Wake me up in a thousand years, a million. Frankly, don't bother to wake me at all.

Sirens spin outside the house. Ambulance, police. Furies unleashed, off they fly. The doorbell is ringing. How dare he? The cell jingling its generic song; like a fool, she thought she'd want to know. She does know. She's always known. Now everyone should leave her alone.

"Su-san!"

She hears him shouting, covers her ears. I don't have to let you in.

He tries the side door to the kitchen, grasping the shiny gold door-knob and twisting it so hard his hand cramps. The kitchen is dark. The door is locked. If Susan won't let him in, he'll have to get Higgs's men to break down the door. Is that what she wants? To be dragged out, drugged, *forced* to abandon ship?

The blinds on the bedroom window above his head come down slat by tilted slat; they clatter awkwardly like falling tim-ber, erasing Susan's black shape pressed against the naked glass. "Susan!" He waves his arms, wishing he had a semaphore and flares in both hands. "It's Jeff! Open up!"

If she hears him, or sees him, she pretends she doesn't.

Jeff pulls out his cell phone. It rings and rings. "Pick up," he mutters. "Pick up the damn phone."

And then, just as he is about to disconnect, he hears a faint click, and a wash of breath. "Susan."

"Please. No."

"Listen."

"No."

"Christopher's been—" He's about to say "located," but he remembers she hates that kind of talk. "Found. Dead."

She freezes. He knows this even though he can't see her. He knows that even Susan, despite her logic, her restraint, is powerless to withstand the plunge into shock. A trance some never wake from. It's nearly always the same.

"Open the door for me, Susan."

She does not answer, but he can hear something through the phone—the faintest squeak of the stair, receiving her weight. A squeak and another and another. A good tracker can find the next track beyond a break without looking, can read the whispered sign. Now he must guess which door will open, side or front. He won't get a second chance. She will open the door a crack, and if he's there, she will let him in, and if he's not, she won't.

Think about what you know about this woman. Think about what you've learned. *Love her. Be her.* Side or front? And it comes to him. Oh, it comes to him like a vision, an angel. He stays at the side door, just stays put, trusts her to materialize because he's just realized that *she trusts him*, and yes, there she is. She opens the door and reaches for him with thin arms. Her skin feels soft as silk as her arms slide around his neck, and she lays her head on his chest and weeps.

He is shaking. He does not want her to see him shaking, but she sees. A grown man is shaking at what he's heard and must divulge. A man who has presumably heard everything. She takes a deep breath and feels her scientist self rising in her like a ghost, all curiosity and detachment, traits for which she has been amply rewarded in this lifetime. "Where?"

"The woods off Blind Hill."

"How far?"

"Half a mile."

She watches him close his eyes for a moment, summoning something. Words? Patience? "I don't know how to tell you."

"He's dead."

Jeff shakes his head. "Something's wrong. They found kerosene, matches scattered nearby—Detective Reddin's already up there. A team out of Albany—"

"I don't get—"

"He's burned, Susan. Real bad."

Susan gasps. The room has become vaporous, the countertops, cabinets a wavering mirage.

"Okay. Try to breathe through your nose. Nice and slow. Let's keep you from passing out."

She listens to his words, tries to obey, sitting down, but her heart is a galloping pump, heaving hard against her chest, against her will. In her mind, a seated pinecone bursts into flame. "How do you know it's Christopher?"

"You described him."

"But you say you found a man who's burned. How burned? How can you tell it's Christopher? It might not be—"

"His sneakers."

"Are you kidding?"

"And the wedding ring. I'm sorry."

"The wedding ring?"

"His wedding ring. Yours. What you described. Gold and silver. Double-twisted. Higgs described it."

Her head sinks into her hands, her elbows propped on the table. "God. God. God." Her mind is like a flapping sail. She cannot stop her tongue. And for a tiny moment she understands how a single word can stand for all the others.

Then, looking up from her cradled hands: "Get a forensic

anthropologist. Right away. I know somebody. We have to study this. Right away. Don't let anyone move him. I'm coming."

"A team's on its way out of Albany."

"All right. I'm going." She is on her feet and reaching for her coat and the boots lined up against the kitchen wall.

"Whoa, Susan."

"I'm going. Now. You take me. Now. I have rights. And I'm prepared to defend them."

"I understand, but you don't need to go. You'll be called—"

No, no, no. She won't abandon him this time. "I'm going."

"They won't let you."

"Yes, they will."

So they set off. She and Jeff. Just the two of them. Trudging past the others, chatting, smoking, in the still, cold air. Well trained, they watch but do not speak, even to Jeff, who signals them with his eyes. They leave the edge of the road, swing onto a deer track that leads into the woods. He did not get too far, Jeff said. But headed in the opposite direction of where they searched. Into the forest and over the frozen snow, broken here and there by the men's heavy boots.

She cannot walk properly. For two steps the crust holds; then breaks. Burning splinters of snow drive into the backs of her calves. After a few minutes, the sock on her right foot has worked its way down below the arch. A blister is forming. She curses herself for her choice of socks, curses the blister and the cold, curses Jeff, whose faith in her is absurd.

But she won't ask him to slow down. She won't complain out loud. She's afraid that if she does, Jeff will have his excuse to turn back, that she will next see Christopher in the overheated front room of the local funeral parlor.

She is not good on trees. She wishes she'd studied them better. These are tall trees, evergreens, a grove as neatly patterned as the forests of Europe and fluttering with pink ribbons. Her fingertips are freezing and she needs to pee and would think nothing of pulling down her drawers, squatting in the snow, if it weren't for Jeff.

Perhaps reading her mind, he quickens his pace, moves farther ahead. Either that or he's trying to lose her, Susan thinks. With stealth, she bends over, pretending to examine something on a nearby boulder, then quickly squats and does her business. If Jeff turns around, tough beans.

Susan's hypothesis was correct, Jeff thinks. Wiry Christopher found a deer path, slender as a turnstile, between two hawthorns. As they pass through these gates, the thorns sticking an elbow, an ankle, he is careful to hold branches back until she is safely through. A Boy Scout's etiquette that she does not acknowledge. All the time, he is listening to her breathing, which shortens as they work their way up the dense hill.

The unseasonable blooms of the searchers' ribbons glow in the afternoon light, but still the way is hard going. The forest floor is a tangle of downed branches, rocks, shards of bark, and here and there, the upstart maple, the flaking silver birch. Every few yards, they stop to catch their breath and sight the next ribbon. Susan is quick to find them, and when she does, she plunges ahead. Without wavering, she swings her bearings on that fluttering pink, a woman possessed.

Then he catches up to her, passes her again. He guesses he can play this game for a little while—it seems to keep her going. His knees by this time are on fire—a pain so intense he finds himself *hee-heeing* through it, using butterfly breaths like the ones Leanne practiced before the baby was born. If his knees were to lock up like they sometimes do, Susan would have to wait by him or go for help. Would she do that? He's not sure.

Suddenly he's aware that she's fallen behind. He turns to see her resting her back against a boulder; her head sunk, her hands on her knees.

"Susan?"

The cold has started tears in her eyes; her nostrils weep. As he approaches her, she shakes her head, waves him on, impatient for her solitude. He sighs, hoping she can hear his exasperation. *Strange woman.* A few paces on, he stops. Her black back is to him, but he can tell what's happening by the way she's hunkered like a raven in the snow. As she straightens, she waddles a step, then turns her fierce expression to him as if to say, *I knew you were there.* Nixing the hearty wave, he pretends to have seen nothing.

He waits for Susan to catch up. Above him, on a branch, a crow caws a comment that Jeff can't interpret. For a second doors slide back and a million thoughts swarm in, a million worries — *Leanne, Corey, Jimmy D.* Doors shut. Susan faces him, panting. He offers her a drink from his army canteen, which he always takes to the field.

Even under these conditions, Susan's gestures have an elegance he can't fathom. She moves with the deliberateness of a heron, he thinks. Neck, throat, arms. A wader, a glider.

The metal threads of his old canteen press against her lips like a kiss. Two smooth gulps and she hands it back to him with a nod of thanks. She's still breathing hard from her exertions; her cheeks blaze pink. "Nothing could survive this cold," she says.

She means no one, of course, but he isn't going to correct her.

A hundred yards away, a group has formed. Men in orange suits; men in black. A yellow ribbon banding the trees warns them not to trespass. Susan takes his arm with barely any pressure, and they stand there, shoulder to shoulder, just looking.

A generator has been set up and a stand of lights. Seeing them, Susan shields her eyes, thinking, no doubt, that the newspeople are here.

He touches her arm. "Forensics is taking photographs."

She nods.

Detective Reddin strides over to them, waving his arms, shouting at them to "hold up." He's wearing rubber gloves and pinching a clear plastic bag between his thumb and forefinger. He's livid. Jeff can see it in his face.

"You can't be here! What the hell do you think you're doing?"

Jeff clears his throat. The man is not much taller than he, but in his irritation he seems to have puffed to twice his size. "Dr. Hunsinger insisted on coming out here for an ID."

"Are you crazy? You don't want to see this."

Jeff feels a hand on his back and realizes that Susan cannot speak.

"She's a tough customer, Detective. She feels she can handle it."

The body bag is in place, a black slug of a shape, smaller than Susan can fathom, a seal's slippery length, an ill-folded tent on an island of scorched grass. The heat of the fire must have melted the snow away. To her surprise, investigators have already arrived, men in orange vests and gloves, holding plastic bags, stooped over like old men hunting bits of treasure in the sand.

The men see her and freeze. All but one. Detective Somebody-or-other comes running, waving his arms above his head to signal her, to warn her off.

Who is the detective screaming at? Susan wonders. Jeff? The others? Doesn't much matter. She feels the way she does when she performs her microsurgeries, an eerie, endorphin-filled calm, and the whole of her attention focused on the task. She shakes off Jeff's arm, stepping across the short stretch of frozen snow to the black bag. The other men move away, finding things to do at the edge of the periphery, yet all the time watching her.

Detective Reddin blocks her path. His shoulders are navy and woolen. His breath is smoke. "I can't authorize this," he says.

"I'm his wife. I'm a *scientist*. I need to see him."

"It's a mistake."

"*My* mistake."

Before this, the worst he'd ever seen Stateside was a call a couple years back. A girl in a bar, having a drink. Her ex-husband and a friend, drinking at the other end of the bar. The girl wasn't much interested in the ex's new motorcycle, but he's got to show it off. When she leaves the bar, he leaves, too. On the road, he's behind her. Then in front of her, playing chicken down the icy road. Finally, he passes her, going 90 on the curve, a gesture staining itself, point made.

He was holding the sobbing girl like a father when Higgs came up fresh from the accident scene. "Got ourselves a headless horseman," he said. And the girl looked up and got it. In the midst of all that, she got it.

He wanted to shoot Higgs. Or the girl—to put her out of her misery.

It's different here. Susan *needs* to see. Jeff steadies himself behind Susan and Reddin, the heel-toe pace of a man processing down a church aisle. His heart is fluttery, his breathing shallow. *If Christopher's in that bag, he's dead.* A weird giddiness twitches his lips. He had a friend in the army who used to laugh at funerals. Couldn't help it, he said. Eulogies worked on him like helium: no matter how tragic the situation, his head filled, his ears, his chest, and the more he held it in, the worse it became until he had to pull his coat over his head and run out of the church or stride purposefully away from the grave site to explode in the backseat of a strategically parked car.

"Why bother to go?" Jeff asked him.

The friend stared. "Respect."

That's it, Jeff thinks. *Susan's got to pay her respects.* Blades whirl in his gut and his head pounds. It's been hours and hours since he's eaten. "The legs," he once heard a marathoner say, explaining why he collapsed within sight of the finish line. "No more legs." That's what it feels like now. He sways on locked legs; his hip joints are banded in iron, his knees numb.

In the silent air, the body bag's zipper sings out in a throaty voice. The sides of the bag gape, and Susan, Reddin at her elbow, bends over the opening like a surgeon examining a wound. One glimpse and her stomach rises, filling her throat with bile. Nothing in this life has prepared her for this transformation, for this revolution of the earth. This is not Christopher. This cannot be Christopher. A corpse looks up at her, unseeing, eyes unholy white in the thick black skull. Where the cheeks should be, valleys, sunken, sucked, vacuumed from inside. Where the nose should be, an ancient ridge. Lips of cellophane bare a row of front teeth. *His* teeth. Unmistakable. How she remembers watching the higgledy-piggledy front teeth that defied years of childhood braces sink into an apple's flesh, then pull away, leaving ragged wounds. "It's him!" she shouts in case they can't hear her. "Him!" She flings it over her shoulder as she turns. She is walking as fast as she can. Not easily or well. Like a deer dragging a broken leg. She's floundering. Not sure of where she's heading or which direction will take her home.

TWENTY-SEVEN

HAVE YOU EVER BEEN LOST? SHE ASKED JEFF, BUT OF COURSE she had been thinking of herself.

The beginning of the trip had been lovely. Flight connections made on time; the chartered sloop anchored at its mooring; the hotel simple but clean. The island was exactly what they'd been looking for. Small. Not overrun. Not a true tourist destination. No beaches. No white sand. Nothing but rain forest and hiking and the sail on the rented boat to and from the big island. It was a real vacation, and what Susan wanted more than anything was peace and quiet after a hectic semester.

Buoyed by all of this perfection, they made love on arrival in the evening and again in the morning, and finally, after a lunch of ripe papaya and pineapple and deeply hued slices of a magenta fruit that stung the tongue with its mixture of sweet and sour, they were ready to take on the day.

Just as they were about to leave their hotel room, Susan faced Christopher, bedecked as usual with camera and tripod, and said, "How about we just take our feet for once, and live the moment unencumbered?"

Christopher smiled. "If that makes you happy."

Susan wore shorts and hiking boots, a floppy hat, and sun-glasses that hugged her temples like glasses for the blind. Around her neck, she'd rolled and knotted a red bandanna to keep insects from making it down her T-shirt. "It actually does."

The hotel owner had supplied a map, but by the time they reached the trail head a few miles down the road, Christopher discovered he'd left it behind in the pocket of the windbreaker Susan had persuaded him he did not need.

Susan grumped and harrumphed at his stupidity, but Chris-topher shrugged it off with a good-natured grin. "This time *you* have to accept some blame."

"Nonsense," she replied. "You shouldn't have to be reminded. You're not a child."

But one step into the moist air of the forest and Susan's irrita-tion disappeared. With one step, she felt as though she'd joined the magnifications under her microscope. Every detail seemed bigger, in brighter focus. The smell of fecund earth, a hundred times more powerful than any forest scent she'd ever smelled. The clotted air. The density of living things. The sounds—a thou-sand birds, crying and singing, not one that she could identify. And other sounds—insects whirring, buzzing, gnawing; monkeys chattering and complaining.

On either side of the cinnamon-colored path rose enormous ferns, if they were ferns, giant plants with huge platterlike leaves, and huge, barrel-trunked trees that shot up into nowhere, their tops lost in the sky.

They had to remove their sunglasses. In the forest it was twilight, twilight punctured here and there with shafts of sparkling light.

"Oh God, it's marvelous." She had to shout to be heard over the birds and monkeys and God knew what else causing this hedonistic roar of exuberance.

"Yes," Christopher breathed. "Paradise."

They linked hands and grinned at each other like children bound by a delicious secret. The forest was enchanted. No other word for it. *Enchanted.*

Everywhere Susan and Christopher looked were orchids and wildflowers and friendly little racer snakes crisscrossing their path. Monkeys peeked down at them, iguanas and lizards skittered and froze at the sides of the trail. Susan yearned to collect but decided not to. This was time to be with Christopher. Really be with him. She had a sense, though he hadn't said so, that Christopher had felt neglected by her these last few months. She'd been so busy with grant applications; graduate school recommendations; her own research. He had been busy, too, of course; but in order to get her work done, several times she'd had to forgo mutual social occasions or tell Christopher to take Molly as his date to this or that performance for which they had subscription tickets.

They lost track of time. Lost track of the light which filtered as ocher—not quite cuing morning or afternoon. So deeper and deeper they went. Paths crossed paths, paths branched, paths serpentined and curlicued. None, it seemed, were marked.

It took several hours for their jollity to wear off. But eventually it happened; they awakened.

Christopher stopped in the middle of a crossroad. A cross path, rather. He took off his hat, the terry-cloth porkpie that Susan detested because it made him look old, and wiped the back of his wrist across his forehead. At this moment, he did look old. Dirt had settled in the creases of his nostrils and of his forehead, darkening them, etching them in his pale face, and the sweaty material of his shirt clung to his back and shoulders, emphasizing a slight stoop.

Susan offered Christopher her water bottle. "Want a slug?" He accepted gratefully, tipping the bottle up and back. She watched his Adam's apple thrusting in rhythm with each swallow. "Hey, leave some."

He nodded, handing the bottle back to her as he wiped his mouth on the back of his hand. "Do you know where we are? I don't."

Susan, having taken her own long drink, stared at him. "You're the navigator," she said.

Christopher shook his head. "I'm lost."

"Not really."

They looked at each other. Twenty-five years of marriage snapping back and forth between them as though each held corners of a wafting sheet.

"Hansel and Gretel. And no bread crumbs," Christopher said. "From what I remember of the map, I thought we were headed north and eventually we'd hit the road. We haven't."

"What time is it?" Susan asked.

"Eight," Christopher said.

"Eight o'clock at night! Can't be."

"Unless my watch is off."

Susan looked at her own wristwatch. "Eight. Impossible, and I'm ready to drop. Right here."

"Here?" Christopher tapped the toe of his boot across the bed of dried leaves at the base of the tree as though testing the strength of floorboards.

Susan nodded and Christopher shrugged. His usual, amenable self. "Not such a bad idea. In the morning we can observe where the sun rises . . ."

Around them, the forest struck up its nighttime music as wild and fathomless as the sounds she used to listen to as a young girl, the sounds of her parents' parties that wafted up through the floorboards and the vents of her room as she tried to fall asleep. But now a calmness that bordered on utter joy stole over her as Christopher spooned his body around hers and she could feel the heat of his belly on her back and the tops of his thighs against the backs of hers.

"Wouldn't this be a perfect time to die?" she asked.

Christopher pulled his arms around her. "No," he said. "I like being alive."

In the morning, mosquitoes buzzed, harmonica-like, around their ears. Susan unrolled her bandanna and covered her hair. Christopher mashed his hat down on his head and remembered a chocolate bar he'd stuck in the pocket of his shorts.

They stretched, they yawned, they gobbled down bits of crumbled chocolate. Then Christopher spotted a blaze on a rock. In the evening light, it had been too dark to see that the trail *was* marked, after all, way down low and quite haphazardly.

"Hallelujah," said Susan.

Christopher grinned, pleased to have solved the problem. "Now in the Arctic, this would have been impossible, you know, without a compass. I can remember once in the corps coming awfully close to getting lost. There was a whiteout . . ."

Susan had heard the story many times—how Christopher had used a torch to keep the compass face from freezing over as he and his comrade marched blindly through the snow, how his unflappable good sense had saved their lives. But now she heard, she thought, what he had been really trying to tell her during all of those iterations, that he had faced his own death and had overcome his fear, that he had been as aware of the reality of the blankness as he was of the revealing light, that he had been lost and, finally, found.

She listened happily now as they tramped along, cooing her admiration, not once losing track or interrupting. The path was clearly leading somewhere. The morning sun was beginning to shine through.

Before long they found themselves out of the rain forest and at the edge of the black macadam road that led to town.

TWENTY-EIGHT

It's almost four-thirty when Jeff steps out of the forest and onto the salt-crusted road. About an hour earlier the sky had closed over and snow had begun to fall in large, downy flakes of celestial eider. Suddenly, there is Higgs, a one-man welcoming committee, offering a handkerchief and a thermos of coffee, which Jeff accepts with a nod, brushing off thoughts of what it might mean for his gut. Susan traveled to the hospital in the back of the ambulance, clinging like a barnacle to the side of the bag which held Christopher's body as though she feared she might lose him again, and no one, not even Reddin, tried to pry her off.

"We're taking a ride," Higgs says. He's wearing his trooper jacket and his trooper hat covered with something that looks like antler velvet. One hand rests on the top rim of the passenger door, which he holds open for Jeff like a chauffeur.

Jeff shrugs and slides onto the vinyl seat. "What's up?" he asks, though he's so damned tired and his knees ache so badly that it hardly matters. He's still got to check the e-mail on Corey, pick up his car.

"Herman Byer called."

"I already—"

"We got us a runaway."

"Shit."

Higgs starts the car. "Have you got any idea where we should look?"

Jeff closes his eyes. The image of a field pops up in his mind. Byer's back field runs up to the ridge, hooks up to the fire road, dead-ends at the top. Where would he run to if he were Corey? The old fire tower not far from Herman's place. "Let's head for Grunson Hill. You know where I mean."

The fire tower was closed now, but that didn't prevent kids from figuring out how to get in. Black, spray-painted graffiti marked the walls beneath the shattered windows, and beer cans and butts of countless cigarettes lay scattered across the floor. The last time Jeff poked his head up there, he'd seen a mattress and an old enamel pot in the corner. Pulling himself up through the trap, he stood and looked out over the fall forest and remembered the thrill of visiting the fire watchers as a boy. Vigilant as raptors, they stood at the windows, their binoculars raised, hunting for signs of smoke. He'd mimicked them, using a pair of binoculars they lent him. One time, he'd spotted something, a light wisp rising in a slender ribbon from a hill. He pointed, excited, convinced that only his superfine eyes had the power to detect it. The watchers came up behind him, but they didn't have to raise their binoculars to see what he was seeing. "Oh that." They laughed. "Spot that a hundred times a day. The dump."

As fire inspector, he could have recommended pulling the tower down, but didn't. The fire tower road is filled with aspen and elderberry, chokecherry, and thickets of crimson cane. In winter, only deer use the road, perhaps addled old men, and boys on the run from themselves.

They start up the steep incline, pocked with boot holes and

scattered with splayed bouquets of fir needles, knocked off their limbs by the searchers' heads and shoulders and elbows. Jeff spits into the snow. *Should've locked down a car here in the first place, might have caught Christopher, instead of letting those assholes chew up the trail.* Ahead of him, Higgs trudges, pushing aside low branches, jerking to reclaim his jacket sleeve from a cluster of thorns. His smooth-soled trooper boots slide back with each step and his cuffs ride up his calves, revealing bare skin.

His ankles are going to blister, Jeff thinks. *Fool.* He lets Higgs gain some distance. Let him have the thrill of the chase. Jeff pulls off a glove and licks a finger, which he jabs in the air. They're downwind of anyone or thing above them. Lowering his hand, he sees he, too, has been pricked. Unawares. Like Sleeping Beauty. One luxuriant tear of his own bright blood bursts from the tip of his index finger, which he licks, savoring for an instant the mixture of sweetness and iron.

Higgs stops to unbutton his jacket, loosen his tie. When he spies Jeff, he turns away, pulls out his radio.

"Ask for warm milk, blankets," Jeff says. "We're going to need them if we find him." He wishes he had a thermos of something other than coffee right now. The snow is still falling, sticking to his hat, his coat, but there's only a light wind. A blessing.

Bending forward, he cups his kneecaps, cradling them in his gloved hands like tiny heads. Someone once told him that inside everyone is the power to heal oneself, an inexhaustible river of energy circuiting the body with the intensity of fire. To draw from it, you have to believe. And here was the difficulty, Jeff thought. "Higgs."

Higgs cocks his head, and Jeff points uphill. What they see coming through the snow—a boy in a flannel shirt, his cuffs flailing at them with the high tense flap of a crow, and jeans and carrot-colored work boots. No hat. No gloves that Jeff can see.

"What the fuck?" Higgs says, throwing down his radio and drawing his gun.

"Whoa," Jeff says. "Easy. It's just the damn boy."

And that is true, though the boy, seeing the gun, freezes.

"Lost?" Jeff asks.

The boy blinks. His face is stained, his lips crusted. A hedgehog fringe of short dark hair sticks up at his crown.

"Corey?"

The boy shakes his head.

"It's Jeff Herdman. Don't be stupid. I know you."

In the car, they turn up the heat to full blast, and Jeff wraps his coat around the near frozen boy then stretches out on top of him. One lost, one saved. Even with the jacket between them Jeff can feel the cold pressing into his thighs, his belly, the boy's body jerking and quaking beneath him. Jeff holds him harder, inhales the vapors rising from his thawing sleeves. The boy smells of kerosene, of ice; his lips are the blue of children who have been swimming too long in the cold water. He wants to kiss them, he wants to tell Corey how much he loves him for being alive. Instead he tents the boy's mouth with his hands and blows into the cavity.

Beneath him, the boy moans and twitches in the places where the warming blood sparks brushfires of pain. Jeff grimaces. He knows what the boy is going through. It is the price you pay for coming back.

TWENTY-NINE

THE DAY JEFF SAW LEANNE AT THE GROCERY STORE AND SAT
with her in the back, she did most of the talking. Mostly she complained: of the customers who were rude to her, of the boss's boss
who had it out for her, of how cold she was from shuttling beer
and bologna and packages of bacon from the cold storage to the
cases. "Takes me hours to get warm," she said, putting down her
cigarette to hug herself against a shiver, then picking it up again.

He wanted to take her hands in his, but something told him
not to. Instead he peeled off his sweater, navy blue, V-necked, and
thrust it at her. "Here."

Leanne took a drag on her cigarette, frowning at the pile of
sweater on the table as though it were an offering of roadkill. "I
ain't going to wear that thing," she said, shoving the sweater back
across the table at him.

"Why not?"

"It's gross is why not. Got your BO."

"Suit yourself." He shrugged.

"Plan to."

Jeff swept up the sweater, making a show of sniffing its armpits
before he slipped it back on.

"Gr-r-r-o-o-ss." Leanne glanced up at the wall clock behind him. "Shit." She stamped out her cigarette and stood up, brushing orange crumbs from her apron lap while she chugged the rest of her soda. The empty can rang dully as she set it down on the table.

"Leanne—" He stood up, too. To do what? Stop her? Kiss her?

Leanne must have wondered, too. Her expression changed swiftly. With her curled lip and hooded eye, she looked like a dog about to bite.

Instead she handed him the soda can. "Wanna redeem something? Take this."

She tried to tell me, Jeff thinks. In her own way, she tried.

There is only one hospital in this town. A child's pile of blocks stacked neatly into the hillside. Dull brick and steel. The subterranean halls of the emergency wing live in permanent twilight, a dusky fluorescence caused by yellowing tubes, flickering current, and gray, enameled walls that remind Jeff of caves.

This is the place where Leanne delivered their son; on an upper floor, an aerie compared to this part of the hospital. But just being in this place makes him shaky and he feels a ghost of himself breaking into a run down a slippery floor, past beds on wheels and IV poles and nurses frowning like hall monitors as he rushes past. Somewhere near the top of this building, in a corner room vibrating with the brightness of a supermarket, his son lies, swaddled like a tiny mummy against his mother's breast.

As soon as they pull up at the entrance to the ER, two EMTs come running. Jeff steps aside as one of them slips Corey from the backseat onto a backboard as deftly as a host slips ice from a tray.

"He's gone hypothermic," Jeff says. "You need to take care of that."

Meanwhile Higgs is talking to someone on his cell. When he snaps it shut, he grunts. "We're going to charge him," he says.

"Charge him with what?"

"You smell the kerosene on that kid? He reeked. And with his record—"

"Ruled innocent."

Higgs coughs into his fist. "It's going to get heavy. You need a ride back to your car?"

Jeff nods. "I need to check on Dr. Hunsinger."

He's just about to get back into Higgs's car when he hears his name. It's Susan stepping through the sliding doors of the ER. She must have been waiting for him.

Higgs toots an impatient honk on his horn. Jeff frowns, watching her come toward him. In only a few hours, their relationship has entirely altered, and who is he now? Friend? Counselor? Stranger? What will she decide?

When she reaches him, she stops, uncertain. Her eyes have the fixed brightness of a person in shock, a glassiness that seems to throw back any light the world has to offer. "Are you leaving?"

Is he? "Long day. How about you?"

"I can't leave yet," she says. "I can't leave him alone."

Thirty

He got up from the kitchen table swiftly, gracefully, like those deer springing from their sleeping place, aroused instantly by the scent of man. He headed for the door off the kitchen, the mudroom door, but he knew they wouldn't be after him. His grandfather's hip was bad; his grandmother wanted him to go.

In the shed, the can of kerosene stood where he'd left it, beside the box of matches.

A light snow had fallen, changing everything. Now light covered dark, dark subdued by light, now something hopeful, like sugar. The snow rested in the crooks of the branches, on the tops of the hay mounds and the crest of the barn.

Already the sun was shining again.

In the woods beyond the house, the sky was a stark and cloudless blue. There would be footprints to trace in the new-fallen snow, but Corey did not think of this. He thought of how sharp and clean the air felt on his cheeks, he thought of how much he liked the smell of kerosene and the feel of matches. He liked that he knew a path that no one else seemed to know. It wasn't a hard path to follow. A simple path, at least to him.

Past the old foundation and the dump, past the rusted springs that rose from the forest floor, past the stand of birches bleeding their bark, past the pile of beer cans glowing faintly green under the snow. Just a bit farther and there he lay.

Snow rested on the pine branches covering the folds of the man's tan pants, on the pine needles covering the folds of his coat. Snow dusted the man's large head, his hair as white as the snow. The man had a disease, the paper said. He couldn't remember who he was or where he came from. How he got where he was. He wished he had that disease. He remembered too many things. He still knew his name and where he came from. He still saw his brother's grin and his mother's sad face. He still saw the house in flames and no place to hide.

"They'll be coming for you," he said aloud. "Coming for to carry me home." A song his mother sang when he was little. How would they come for him? he wondered. With handcuffs and guns? With a long white jacket with locking arms? He'd seen one on a show. A man wrapped in a locked jacket and chains, dumped in the sea to die. But somehow he got out of them and back to the top. He didn't know how.

He wanted to tell them that it wasn't his fault. But they wouldn't believe him. He just wanted to tell them that he found the man and felt sorry for him, that the man was running just like him, that he was running and got tired and lay down to sleep. That's what happens when you've been running a long time, when your legs hurt real bad and your lungs hurt, too. That's what happens when you don't know where you're going or why—you just head for the woods because the woods are safe. He felt sorry for the man because he got lost, and then he got dead, but he couldn't just leave him here, because he'd be blamed.

The shiny cap dropped into the snow as Corey hoisted the can, the heavy can, which slipped and bucked in his hands, gushing kerosene more in one place than another until the can was empty.

His fingertips were soaked.

He'd been good, he told the old man. He'd stayed out of trouble. Only one accident and he'd stripped the bed himself and rinsed the place on the sheet in the tiny sink. No fires. His hands were clean. He hadn't done nothing. He'd hardly said a word. But he'd heard his grandmother talking downstairs at night. She couldn't sleep since he come. She was always afraid.

A home, she said. A place for boys like him.

The blue had drained from the sky, leaving a white blanker than snow. No wind. Even so, the first match flamed yellow and died. The second, too. But the third blazed and held steady.

He listened to the faint crackle of the matchstick as the flame traveled toward his fingertips, gathering strength, gathering heat, bursting to meet his flesh.

He kneeled and touched one match to the hem of the kinked shoelace, another to the edge of a soaked sleeve, yet another to the man's collar. He felt like a little boy, saying his prayers. Then around and around the body he went, lighting here and there. His heart felt like warm butter in his chest; his head filled with joy. *You haven't done bad,* he said. *Not like me. It ain't your fault you died.*

THIRTY-ONE

THEY FIND SEATS IN THE FAR CORNER OF THE CAFETERIA, which to their relief is emptying of orderlies and nurses and doctors on their dinner breaks. To Susan those diners look like kids at a summer camp, hunched toward each other across the tables like kids with secrets. She is grateful that she has Jeff, just Jeff. She doesn't have to tell her secrets to anyone else. Aside from Detective Reddin and the doctor in charge of the morgue, she has not spoken to anyone since Christopher was found in the woods. Oh yes, and that reporter who showed up to ambush her in the waiting room, whom she deflected with one well-aimed glare and a brandished palm. The old Susan. Ferocious, effective. Have to thank her for showing up.

But now, sitting across from Jeff, she can barely find her voice, let alone her toughness. "Where have you been? What have you learned?"

Jeff picked up a hamburger in line. I need protein, he said. She nodded, aping him, though she didn't intend to eat a bite of the flaccid-looking meat in the cottony bun; she was simply grateful to follow, to have someone to lead her through the motions of normal behavior. When Jeff reached for a carton of milk, she did, too. When he reached for a slice of cake, she did, too. When it came time to pay, she tried to wave him off, fumbling in her coat pockets for her wallet, but not in time. He pulled out a credit card, shook his head at the cashier's query, was he an employee? Susan noticed that the cashier gave him a discount anyway. They had that kind of look, Susan thought, of people who really need a break.

Now here they are. Jeff is staring at the layers of bun and burger as though regarding a geological formation. He puts the burger down, sips his milk instead. And meanwhile she is simply waiting. She knows that if she is patient, Jeff will speak, he will tell her what's on his mind.

"You remember I was concerned about a kid?"

"A kid?"

"The boy who was getting kicked out of his grandfather's place. One of *my* kids."

Her mind suddenly jumps. A fire starter. She leans in closer. Her heart, which hasn't been beating properly, she's certain, since she saw Christopher in the woods, starts up again too fast. "You called him from the house."

Jeff nods. "I called the grandfather. Corey's guardian."

Corey. Makes her think of a song, white coral bells. "You said the man was a jerk."

Jeff grimaces. "Yeah, I did. Well, after you got in the ambulance with Christopher, I got a call that Corey had run away from home. He'd been missing since around noon—"

Jeff is looking at her hard. It's a clue, she thinks. But what kind of clue?

"We picked him up on Grunson Hill—"

Grunson Hill? What's that? Why's he telling her this? Why is he tangling things when she needs them straight?

"He'd gone hypothermic, no jacket, gloves, hat." Jeff stares at his hamburger again. Does it know the secret? "The boy was soaked in kerosene."

Later she will think about those words and wonder at her first thought, which was relief that the boy had escaped the madman who set Christopher on fire. An image leaped to her mind of two hostages—one sacrificed, one fated to slip free. In the end, wasn't it better that the boy had lived?

But Jeff continued. He was saying that the police were going to charge the boy, that the fire starter might have struck again. He was saying that the boy might have set Christopher on fire.

It seemed then as if the whole world had defied the laws of nature, that God had given a swift kick to the globe to get it spinning faster than it had ever spun before and that she and all the earth's inhabitants had launched into thin air.

PART III
EPILOGUE

Sailing Backward

She meets Jeff at the Cup these days. A morning or two a week. He looks well, she thinks. He seems to be taking better care of himself, perhaps even eating some of the diet she recommended, something she researched online. She suspects, too, that he has a woman, that a tide has turned since Leanne left him. He doesn't speak often of his own affairs, though. Corey is still his charge and she is, too, in a way. Jeff's been the liaison between the family court and Hillside Farms, the juvenile detention facility that Corey was sent to, and he's been a one-man support group for her, committed to her recovery. This morning she plans to ask him one more favor.

She's chosen a table by the window, so she can look out for him, and yet it is a surprise when his hand comes down on her shoulder with a light squeeze. He slides into the seat opposite hers. She smiles. Those eyes. If she were younger.

"How's Susan this morning?"

"How's Jeff?" Does he know she's faintly mocking him, though she rather enjoys the thought of being able to answer questions about herself from a seemingly objective third person?

"I asked first."

"Coffee?"

Jeff shakes his head. "Soy milk chai."

"You're not the man I used to know."

Jeff nods. "You're not paying attention."

"I still drink tea. With honey."

While Jeff goes to the counter to place the order, Susan thinks about how to present her plan. It's lunacy, and yet—perhaps Jeff will be grateful. For weeks, he's been trying to find a placement for Corey. Not a foster home in the state will accept him—even the "therapeutic homes" with foster parents trained for difficult cases. Fire starter. Legally, Jeff has to state it. And that, he has told her, ends the call. She wants custody of Corey. Yes. She wants a letter of recommendation from Jeff to Social Services. She's had her lawyer look into it: it seems it's possible. Corey has no one else in the world who's interested in raising him.

The idea took root the first time she visited Corey. She'd gone looking for an explanation and come away with a plan.

The staff person accompanying Corey was a deeply black man wearing pants with pockets that gaped like laboring mouths over his rounded hips. As he approached the open door, he slowed for a moment, a tour guide suddenly remembering an important fact. Then, spotting her sitting alone at the table, he entered, Corey in his wake, pulled by his draft. She could not make him out behind the large man.

"Bruce." He reached to shake her hand.

"Susan." His palm, she noticed, was damp, betraying a nervousness that was not outwardly apparent from his calm manner. Jeff was against this visit. They'd had it out last week. Apparently he was not the one to smooth the way. Apparently he trusted her enough not to mince words. He called her proud, stubborn, lonely. Accusations she couldn't in good conscience deny. I just want to see him, she insisted. I just want to know who he is.

Corey stood slightly back from Bruce's shoulder; together they formed an open hinge. He was wearing a clean white T-shirt and gray sweatpants whose cuffs settled a bit too long on his coffee-colored house sandals. ("Required," Michelle, the director of Hillside, had explained, as Susan's gaze fell on the racks of plastic sandals, each toe pad outlined in the soles. Susan began to slip off her shoes—"Not you," Michelle exclaimed. "Not visitors.")

"Corey," Bruce said. "Mrs. Hunsinger's come to see you." His voice was rough, but not unkind. His gruffness, Susan sensed, was for the boy's own good.

Corey raised his chin a little and looked straight at her with dark eyes. No questioning or surprise in his straight gaze, no malice, either. What had he been told about who she was and why she was here? Susan wondered. And if he did decide to speak, what would she tell him? That she was a scientist? That she had faith in her powers of observation? That she believed she could tell good from bad—the possibility of redemption from true evil?

She could tell him she's a fool.

She looked at the boy, looked and looked while his gaze anchored to a spot on the floor between the empty chair and the edge of the table. He was smaller than she imagined he would be. A slip of a boy, hard muscled, head shaven like a prisoner's. Scars swam up his neck, glistening amoebas that flooded the instant he noticed her looking at them.

"Let's sit down," Susan said. "I'll sit down." She gestured with an open palm to the chairs at the other side of the table. "Please."

Around them other visits were getting under way—each at an identical table. Mothers and grandmothers, it seemed, were the ones who cared. Wide-eyed younger siblings, scrabbling to get closer to the Tupperware being opened, the treat inside revealed.

Silence lasted only a minute with them, then the volume rose abruptly like a room of bidders come to life.

Michelle, whom Susan had thought would join them, was called away for an emergency: a new boy had arrived without his meds, without even a prescription. "What were they thinking?" she asked before she disappeared into her office, a telephone already clamped to her ear.

Corey moved slowly, dropped himself at last into the chair across from Susan. A victory for gravity. Bruce frowned and pulled his chair closer to Corey's.

"Well," Susan said, "this is odd, I know. But I'm happy to see you. I mean that. I'm a strange person that way—I need to know what things look like, taste like, smell like—"

A flicker of alarm passed over the boy's features that showed Susan he was paying attention.

Her hand darted out— "Oh God, the way that sounds! Like I'm going to eat you! Oh dear—" She couldn't help laughing just one embarrassed explosion of air, but it worked. Corey smiled. A wink of light, a fissure in the dead blank of his face, but Susan felt a surge of something—hope? relief?

"I'm babbling," Susan said. "I'm sorry. I was told you don't like to speak, and here I am babbling away at you, and you're probably worried, worried I'm going to shout at you or something. I'm not. I'm here because—well, I read what you wrote—your statement—for the police. I guess I'm confused and would like to understand better—you said you didn't want to hurt my husband. You said he was already dead. You—" She had to pause to catch her breath, or rather wrestle it from a burry tickle that threatened suddenly to close her throat. Her hand flew to her larynx. Choking, on what, though? Her own words? Her mouthful of grief?

Corey tugged Bruce's sleeve and pointed and Bruce jerked straight. "Water?"

Susan nodded and slipped a look of thanks at Corey. Perhaps in retrospect this was when she came to love the boy. Not romantically. That would be idiotic. But if she were here to judge a soul, Corey's attentiveness, his concern would tip the scale.

Once she'd sipped her glass of water, she found herself as mute as the boy who sat staring down at the faint scratches in the varnished wood. She had planned to ask the boy what Christopher looked like when he found him. She couldn't ask that anymore.

Bruce touched Corey's shoulder. "You going to say something? Now's the time. Now's the time to say something. Mrs. Hunsinger hasn't got all day."

Susan wanted to correct this, she wanted to say that she would stay all day, that she had all the time in the world, but she couldn't. In spite of herself, she knew Bruce was right: she was waiting for something with her breath held, her heart beating a rapid, insistent drum. *Tell me you're sorry*, she willed. *That's all.*

The boy's chin dropped again. His lips remained still. Nothing seemed to come to him. Nothing at all.

Bruce shrugged his big rounded shoulders, stood Corey up and turned him around by his. "All right then," he said. "We don't force anyone to talk, even though it would be nice." Nice for them to talk? Or nice to have leave to force them to talk? Susan stood up. No farewell handshakes. Then suddenly something came to her. "Is he allowed chewing gum? Is there a vending machine of any kind?"

Bruce nodded. "It's a privilege, though. Kid's got to earn it."

Susan unsnapped her purse and pulled out a five-dollar bill. "Buy yourself something," she said. "A treat from me. When you earn it." Corey's chin came up and for a second he caught her eye. It was not a look of gratitude, or one of hostility. It was the best look she could have hoped for—a look of pure curiosity.

Jeff is back with glasses of water for both of them, a ceramic mug of black tea for her. "Mine will be up soon," he says. "Someone will bring it over."

"This was Christopher's favorite table. He liked to sit here in the sun. Like a turtle. This was his rock."

Jeff sighs. "What's up?"

Susan lifts an eyebrow. She forgets that he's a tracker. What sign betrayed her this morning?

"The napkin," Jeff says in answer to the unspoken question. "You don't usually pinch your napkin."

The young man who sets the chai on the table beams at them as though they are new lovers.

"Mmm," Susan says. "What a great smell."

"Want some?"

"No. It's that cinnamony smell. Goes perfectly with my tea."

"Shoot."

Susan squeezes her fist into a gavel, knocks the edge of the table once, gently. "I want to adopt Corey."

"Shit, no."

"Yes." Both fists are on the table now, knuckles touching. She's ready to do battle.

"Why?"

"There's no one else. I like him. I have means."

Jeff clasps the handle of his mug, releases it. "Holy cow."

"You'd help, right?"

"Christ."

"I'm under no illusions," Susan says. "I know a woman who adopted a Vietnamese child during the war. Convinced she was saving a life. When the child grew up, she wrote a book, a diatribe against her adopted mother and all those 'white elitist liberals' as she put it, 'colonizers' who'd robbed her of her culture, her birth family, her language.

"I felt terrible for the mother. She'd only done what she thought was best: she loved her daughter. But there it was, the first line of the book: 'My adopted mother killed me the day she brought me home.'"

"Forget politics, Susan, we're concerned about *you*."

"What? I'm educated, healthy." *A little insane.*

"Can you keep up?"

Susan releases her breath in a long, reedy *hah*. "No. I can't. That's why I have you. And others. I'll have plenty of help. And in the event that I die prematurely, Corey will be provided for." Susan leans forward, clasps her mug in both hands and with a confidential look, calculated to draw Jeff in. "Have you ever renamed a boat?"

"Have I ever what?"

"Changed the name of a boat."

Jeff lets out a light puff of exasperation. "I haven't been on a boat since I shipped out to 'Nam."

Susan leans in closer. "There's a ritual. Christopher taught it to me. He had a little sailboat when I met him, and after we were married, he wanted to rename it after me. Silly, but I loved the idea, actually. So here's what you do—"

"And if you don't?"

"Curses, disaster."

Jeff raises his eyebrows. "You call yourself a scientist?"

"Be quiet. First, you get rid of everything on that boat that has the old name—all the scraps of documents, the cocktail napkins, the detritus; next, you sail backward."

"Backward? How do you do that?"

"It's not too hard. You steer across the wind and loose the sails." She can see that day, the heavenly blue of the sky, the perfect breeze. She and Christopher laughing as the wind caught the mainsail and the jib, separating them like wings.

Jeff sips his chai, then wipes his upper lip with his napkin. "Okay. Then what?"

"You celebrate." And they had, popping the cork on a bottle of champagne. "You've let go of the old, and you're ready for the new."

"Susan, the boy comes from complete chaos."

And has a hand in it, too. She knows this. She, herself, is in chaos made worse by the boy's actions.

"He needs a chance to stabilize. He needs consistency. Structure."

"I understand that, and that's what I plan to provide. I'm under no illusions." Ballsy, she can hear Jeff thinking. Dangerous. "Don't you think I can claim a little experience?" Her eyes sting. "I've been through a hell of a lot."

Jeff nods lightly. "That I'll give you."

"This you may not—I believe the boy's act was an act of mercy." Why she believes this she doesn't know. If Jeff were to ask her to explain, she couldn't. Gut instinct. The sort of intuition she's always trusted in herself, the leap, some would call it faith, that has vaulted her over chasms of unknowing to scientific truth.

Jeff shakes his head. "He was fucking desperate, Susan."

Susan closes her eyes. In the statement for the police, Corey wrote that he was scared to tell anyone about finding Christopher. Even though Christopher was already dead, he was scared he'd be blamed like he was blamed for setting the fire that killed his brother. No one would believe me, he said. No one ever does. The autopsy report supports Corey's claim, but no one can explain the care the boy took in lighting those separate fires.

Susan is sitting at the kitchen table, her laptop open, her mug of tea cooling. She is trying to find a way to explain her actions to Peter, who must be told what she is up to. She believes the boy, she wants to write. She even thinks she might understand him. He was scared to tell anyone, so considering the circumstance, he did the logical thing, emptied a gallon of kerosene over the dead man's body and set him on fire.

You can't call that murder, Susan types. *You can't.* And if it were murder, shouldn't she share the charge? Wasn't she the one who failed in her attentions? Who went for a walk when she should have stayed put? Who left the door unlocked? Who deluded herself with the idea that she could go it alone?

I blame myself, not the boy. We are both consumed with guilt.

A few weeks after their meeting at the Cup, Susan brings Jeff with her to visit Corey, and there is a surprise for them: Corey has been named "Youth of the Week" for his exemplary behavior. Michelle is smiling as she greets them in the front hallway of the dormitory. As a reward, she tells them, Corey will be allowed to show them the barnyard on his own, as long as they feel comfortable with that.

"Of course," Susan says, though she does not feel nearly as confident as she knows she sounds.

Corey appears on the stair, Bruce at his elbow. He is wearing the same uniform he wore on the previous visit—the gray sweats and white T-shirt. Today, however, he slips off his sandals and slides on heavy black sneakers, the thick white laces worked out in a sort of froth of cotton over the top of the shoe. Laces, Susan suddenly remembers, were not allowed in the ward where Christopher once stayed.

Bruce hands him a hooded sweatshirt that matches the pants, slaps Corey on the back. "Be cool."

Corey ducks his chin and disappears into the sweatshirt. His bristly crown is all they see before his head pushes through and his cheeks flush. Excitement? Or the exertion of pulling his head through the tight opening? Susan wonders.

The car ride along the narrow lane is brief. Dilapidated arrows and signs point the way to the farmyard, but Susan can hear Corey's breath quicken, the faint creak of the shoulder belt as he leans forward as if to steer them. He doesn't speak, though. Not a word.

The facilities, like the rest of the campus, are on a diminished scale. The sorts of temporary barns and sheds, red with white trim, of a small county fair. On every side, the paint is blistering to reveal the gray boards beneath.

Susan makes a mental note to maintain an even tone, a delighted smile, even. Clearly, Corey is animated by the place, proud in some way that she does not understand. He's only been here a month, but this seems to be the place where he feels at home. Michelle told them he feeds the goats and volunteers to muck the horses' stalls. For this enthusiasm, he earned privilege after privilege. The five dollars is gone.

Corey walks ahead of them toward the henhouse, then waits for them to catch up. When they do, he points to a sign above the door, his small face poised to receive their reaction. The sign, boy-painted on a plywood square, reads: BEWARE OF EVIL CHICKEN. In smaller letters: BEWARE OF ATTACK CHICKEN.

Susan laughs. "Evil Chicken? What'd she do? Peck somebody?"

Corey nods.

"I bet you can teach these boys a lot, Corey," Susan says. "I bet most of them don't know how to handle chickens."

Across from the henhouse is a shed that houses two enormous sows, lazing together on a bed of soiled straw.

Jeff leans his arms on the railing across the door. "They remind me of my aunt Rhoda and her husband, Jules. Fat as them pigs and happy, too."

Susan turns to Corey. "Do you slop the pigs? Do you enjoy it?"

Corey squints, not at her, but across the frozen ground.

Anything she says, he seems to evaluate—a trick question or not? A trap or not? Susan thinks.

Just then, the ducks across the lane catch Susan's eye. "Make way for ducklings!" Indeed, a large brown duck and her ducklings are waddling tipsily down the bank to greet them. "Oh look!" Susan says. "A mohawk." She points to a duckling with a fringe of white down poofed along the scalp.

Jeff smiles. "Check out the 'Fro—" A duckling sporting a bolster of fuzz on his head, pauses in front of Jeff and opens his bill as if to reply.

Susan and Corey look, and laugh, at exactly the same time.

Disturbed, yes. Damaged, yes, I understand, she told the judge. *We're both damaged,* she intoned inside her head. But summoning her most distinguished, professorial mien, she insisted that she understood the situation and understood her responsibilities, that as her ward, Corey would receive psychiatric treatment, private tutors—training in any vocation he might aspire to.

Judge Baner, a middle-aged man with a kind, almost cartoonish face, smoothed his palm back over his balding pate. "You make an offer, Dr. Hunsinger, which is, quite honestly, difficult to refuse."

*　　*　　*

She wonders, Should I buy some toys? No. Pencils, paper, crayon, paint. Paint the walls, she might tell him, paint your cave.

She will buy him his own sheets, a bookcase, a reading light, a flashlight, a compass, a bureau (remembering how excited he was to have his own things). She will buy books, Legos, foam bats, a skateboard, and a scooter. She will buy a bat and ball, a leather glove. How about a microscope and glass slides? Perhaps the boy has never seen the world as a speck grown large. She could show him how to affix a cell from his cheek, how to swab and smear. She remembers the wonder of it, looking the first time, her eye squashed to the metal ring of her mother's microscope; her mother's calm instruction to "keep both eyes open"—she remembers entering another world, breaking the surface of what felt like the true world, her mother and father's world. A cheek cell, a drop of menstrual blood, a strand of hair. Seeing, seeing for the first time. She'd never been the same after.

She will teach Corey to see as she did. *The microscope, portal of possibility, an entrance to another world.*

Later, she sits at the kitchen table and looks at her list and feels appalled. What was I thinking? The boy's nearly thirteen, knows how to light matches, drench a body in kerosene and let it burn. The boy knows what Christopher looked like curled beneath a pine bough in the snow. She is ashamed. A baseball bat. All the better to smash your head in, my dear. A microscope. Her brow sinks to her crossed arms, resting on the table. She weeps.

Still, the gilded cage is better than where he lives now. Isn't it? And Jeff had told her, no foster home in the state will take him.

Straight from Hillside Farms, they drive to the animal shelter. A strange decision, perhaps. Perhaps she is avoiding the finality of driving straight home. Corey has spent several weekends with her since the judge's decision, and they have gone well. But this is it. His small duffel of belongings rests in the trunk. He sits beside her, a quiet presence. But his eyes are big, alight with excitement. Her promise to him was a kitten. His own kitten. A puppy would be too stimulating, too much work, frankly. A kitten, she could handle. Dewy-eyed and soft. Playful. A low-maintenance kitten. A house cat. A luxury item. She knows the boy used to work on his grandfather's farm. He knew all about the care of cows and pigs and no doubt barn cats. But his own kitten. To name. To care for. He smiled at the offer of this. He nodded yes, he wanted to pick out his own kitten.

The kitten room at the shelter is brightly lit and swarming with tiny, fuzzy bodies, some mewing, their mouths opening and closing like baby birds expecting to be fed. Others are frisking, chasing their own tails, clawing furiously on the carpeted post in the center of the room. Susan, though not usually allergic to cats, feels her eyes water, her throat catch. The air is saturated with dander, she thinks. An asthmatic's hell. But Corey does not seem to be affected. He crouches, riveted by the kittens' antics, and Susan can see that shy smile again, the losing of himself in his delight. A kitten in the corner has caught his particular attention. He moves toward it slowly; the kitten, lost in its world, bats a felt mouse, touching its side with a paw, then leaping backward in fear. Forward and back, forward and back. The most insecure confident being Susan has ever seen.

"Slam," Corey says, pointing at the kitten in the corner.

"Slam?" She forgets to be surprised that the boy is talking at all.

"Dunk," he says.

She shakes her head. She doesn't know his language and is suddenly afraid as she used to be when Christopher talked and made no sense. "Slam. Dunk," she echoes. Then smiles. She is the one frozen out of language. "Slam Dunk. Great name. Is he the one then?"

The boy scoops the kitten easily in his right palm, raising her and lowering her suddenly, an elevator sinking fast.

Her mouth tightens, but she remains silent. Slam dunk. That's what he's showing her and what she asked.

"Slam Dunk lives here," she says, pointing to the wicker basket with the red cushion in the corner of the kitchen. "There's her food—" She points to two aluminum dishes lined up at the end of the counter. "Her box is in the bathroom. You scoop once a day."

The boy looks at her.

She doesn't think there is anything wrong with his brain, yet she's unclear as to whether or not he understands her instructions. From the neutrality of his expression, she half expects Bartleby's reply: "I prefer not."

Days go by and the poop is scooped, the bowls filled. When she praises him, he shrugs. Shrugs and shifts his gaze to the floor the way he did the first time they met at Hillside Farms.

Keep your expectations low, Jeff warns her. That's the only way you might find yourself pleasantly surprised. Well, she is surprised—and enormously pleased. She can't remember ever feeling quite so proud or pleased about anything.

And he's begun to talk to her. At first a whisper. Now and again, like the day he met the kitten, full voice. She heard him singing in the shower this morning. It was a song with no words, a cooing like the mourning dove's cry, a pigeon. A strange moment. She was so used to being alone that her first thought was "Christopher." She thought he'd come back.

It occurred to her, later, that she was in an interesting position—first, witness to her husband's disintegrating speech, and now, the only person this boy trusts enough to speak to. He acquires language like a rock climber scaling a wall. He reaches, grasps, grips, then rests. There's something inspiring about the way he heaves himself forward, then pauses, conserving energy, reorienting himself. In his own way, Susan thinks, he's fearless.

The cat seems to thrive on the boy's seemingly indifferent yet steady care. It lies on his bed at night and follows him around the house. "She likes you," Susan remarks aloud one morning. "You feed her." An observation merely, not a dig.

The boy looks down at the cat, but does not attempt to stroke her.

"She likes your smell, too. Something about your essence."

If the boy understands her, he shows no sign of it. He sits down on the sofa and clicks on the TV with the remote. (She had the TV programmed to play nothing but public television.) Today, Saturday morning, two jolly middle-aged men are hammering away on a roof while managing to talk to the camera.

Slam Dunk curls in the boy's lap and licks his fingers with firm purpose. Susan can't help but watch as the cat works around his scarred knuckles and deep into the valleys between his fingers as though she were a nurse with a wet cloth. How Corey's gotten so many scars, she doesn't know. She has to remember to mention them to Jeff when he checks in. He calls every day, sometimes two or three times a day. And each time he greets her, she can hear the uncertainty in his voice, uncertainty edged with relief as if one of these days he expects to find her dead on the floor.

The kitten, growing bold, stretches up the front of Corey's chest, nuzzling and working her tongue around the side of his neck, the base of his ear. And then, just for a second, Susan catches Corey smiling faintly, his eyes still on the hammering, hardworking men.

*   *   *

Susan mixes herself a drink: jigger of Seven Seas; jigger of sweet vermouth; dash of bitters—Christopher's drink. He used to lift his glass, praising the Prohibitionists whose ban on liquor stimulated the imagination to create cocktails in order to disguise rotgut whiskey. He was full of tidbits like that. Word origins. Historical trivia. The trivia of place. Cock tails, though. She'd never questioned that. Tail of a cock, an iridescent feathery thing, prone to swish after a few. Who knew? Or cared.

Corey is asleep; he goes to bed early, eight o'clock, it is important to him. He is proud of this. His early-to-bed, early-to-rise lifestyle. The neatness with which he keeps his things. She sips her cocktail down fast, as she stands, the heel of her palm against the Formica counter. She sips it fast as though the drink were tap water laced with something medicinal, echinacea, fluoride. This drink tastes good and it seems, to Susan, inadequate. She might have to fix herself another. But on draining the glass and reaching for the bottle of whiskey, she revises her opinion. It was adequate. More than. She can walk straight, but she also feels a flood of courage and, strangely enough, clarity.

This morning she received an e-mail from Peter, a long-delayed reply to hers. He's almost reached the coast. They're close enough to hear the sound of the ocean. *He* hears it, but to the Pygmies, who have never heard the sound of an ocean, it's a standing whirlwind, a lion, an enormous chimpanzee. When he told them the ocean tastes like tears, they replied, "But why does the ocean cry?"

In the past she might have scorned such a question, but now it occurs to her that these are the questions that lead to science. That questioning, in any form, is good.

Gliding past the living room, she makes it upstairs, and once seated on the toilet, she realizes that she is, indeed, inebriated. Nothing sloppy. Nothing weepy or silly. A peculiar state. An altered one. She sits and stares at herself in the narrow rectangle of mirror attached to the back of the bathroom door. Not her idea. The cheap mirror, the placement. It came with the house and she had not had the energy to pull it down, putty the screw marks, repaint.

She sits and looks at herself. A woman in the middle of middle age with the black slacks and black knee socks pulled down around her ankles like discarded skin. Her knees stick out, white, bony. Her shinbones are such narrow ridges. The sag of her sweater covers her sex.

She leans forward, propping her elbows on her thighs, fascinated. By her self. Which does not feel like her self at all. Alcohol does this to her sometimes—splits her from her self. Allows her to observe with complete detachment. Like a scientist. Private joke.

She sees with amusement and, yes, some dismay, that she appears older than she thinks she does. Her hair is silver white. Her skin drawn taut from cheekbones to chin, translucent and soft. She is lucky to have her mother's skin, her bone structure. She is relatively unwrinkled for a woman of her age and yet she looks old today. Unmistakably old. Except for her eyes. She smiles at her eyes, marveling at their color, the pale burning blue of moonstones, the icelike clearness of a husky's eyes. Your eyes are jewels, Christopher once said to her. That's not what they mean to her. To her they mean, *Ah. Here you are. You are you. You have always been you. I'm so grateful.*

She grins. In this state, she can see herself sitting on a toilet; a half-crocked woman on the toilet, talking to her self. Her self and her not-self hovering nearby.

You're going through a crisis, she tells herself as if catching up an old friend. *Christopher is dead. Christopher is gone.* The words sound hollow. Christopher has been gone such a long time. Who is she fooling?

At the end of Peter's e-mail was a postscript: *Shit. I forgot. I'm not angry with you. I'm actually rather proud of you. I don't under-stand what you're doing. But I get that it's a miracle.*

Lifting up from the seat, she is careful to avert her eyes. She doesn't want to see herself in the process of. She flushes the toilet. Washes her hands with the lavender soap Jeff told her he liked. Rinses her teeth.

Suddenly she is sober. It is often like that. At the apex of the alcohol's effect, she drops like a stone. She shakes her head. Sighs. *I'm proud of you . . . it's a miracle.* Completely sober. She rather regrets it.

He is almost asleep, his cat curled into his neck like a velvet scarf. Every night her purr makes him happy, makes him sleep easier, though sleep is not easy. Every night he closes his eyes and thinks about his mother. He can see her the way she used to look way back when she might have been happy. They were at the fair, he remem-bers, the carnival side, he and Lance riding rides though they were too little to reach the mark on the post beside the turnstile. He and Lance on the kiddie coaster. It felt like a big coaster to him, like it was a hundred feet tall and made out of sticks. He remembers the jolt of the car when it started, Lance pushing him back onto the seat behind the metal bar. Then they were a train chugging up a moun-tain that it didn't seem they could climb. At the top the train paused like it was tired, and then it leaped forward, and they were flying, dropping, he felt his stomach rise and his scream, too, shooting high up in the air like a hawk's whistle, blasting the sky, and as they came around the turn, he saw his mother. She was waving, up on her tip-toes and her mouth open and her eyes so bright, so proud that he sat up and waved back, waved and waved, pretending he wasn't scared.

Acknowledgments

I WOULD LIKE TO THANK READERS BOTH EARLY AND LATE WHO helped me tremendously in clarifying my vision and making the story richer: Melanie Rae Thon, Elizabeth Bloom, Liz Huntington, Melora Wolff, Ginnah Howard, and Kim Ilowit.

I am grateful to the many experts who shared their knowledge with me and assisted me in my research: Professor of Biology Stanley Sessions of Hartwick College, whose love of the axolotl is unsurpassed; Donelle Hauser, LMSW, who kindly gave me access to the facilities of the Burnham Youth Safe Center in Lenox, Massachusetts, and to her insights on the juveniles residing there; Eric H. Martin, chief instructor, Over the Edge, Inc., for orienting me to the realities of a search-and-rescue mission; Michael Finneran, program director, Otsego County Juvenile Fire Instruction Program, who educated me on the psychology and assessment of juvenile fire starters; the Honorable Judge Brian Burns, who welcomed me to his courtroom and answered my many legal and custody questions; Jim Maloney of the Oneonta Fire Department, who assisted my search for authentic language; Professor of Forensics Dawn Steadman of Binghamton University, who led me through the details of a forensic examination;

and Dr. James Bercovitz, who kept me up-to-date on the latest findings in the neuroscience of Alzheimer's disease.

I thank Sue Standing for the "day of fire" experiment that launched this book. And I thank Johana Arnold, whose wisdom deepened this book.

Miriam Altshuler—who was there for me even after a long hiatus—thank you. Samantha Martin was simply the loveliest and most perceptive editor a writer could have.

Finally, I would like to thank friends and family who have shown their support for this book over the five years of its making: Anne Pollack; Tony Eprile; George, Yvette, and Richard Bercovitz; Elizabeth and Thomas Torak; Nancy and Immanuel Lichtenstein; Sue Straubing and Sandy Bolster—and most helpful of all, Jim, Iris, and Sarah, who so cheerfully bear the brunt of an in-house writer.

About the Author

ALICE LICHTENSTEIN GRADUATED FROM BROWN UNIVERSITY and was named the Boston University Fellow in Creative Writing. She has received a New York Foundation for the Arts Grant in Fiction and has twice been a fellow at the MacDowell Colony. Lichtenstein has taught at Boston University, Wheaton College, Lesley College, and the Harvard University Summer School. She now teaches at Hartwick College in Oneonta, New York.